ANGEL WARRIORS

ANGEL WARRIORS
BATTLE WARRIORS SERIES

Aretha Nesmith

ANGEL WARRIORS
Battle Warriors Series

This is a work of fiction. All of the characters, names, incidents, organizations, and dialogue in this novel are either the products of the author's imagination or are used fictitiously.

iUniverse books may be ordered through booksellers or by contacting:

iUniverse
1663 Liberty Drive
Bloomington, IN 47403
www.iuniverse.com
1-800-Authors (1-800-288-4677)

Because of the dynamic nature of the Internet, any web addresses or links contained in this book may have changed since publication and may no longer be valid. The views expressed in this work are solely those of the author and do not necessarily reflect the views of the publisher, and the publisher hereby disclaims any responsibility for them.

Any people depicted in stock imagery provided by Thinkstock are models, and such images are being used for illustrative purposes only.
Certain stock imagery © Thinkstock.

ISBN: 978-1-4917-1454-6 (sc)
ISBN: 978-1-4917-1456-0 (hc)
ISBN: 978-1-4917-1455-3 (e)

Library of Congress Control Number: 2013920828

Print information available on the last page.

iUniverse rev. date: 07/29/2015

To Curtis Farris and Andy Matovich, who never once stopped me from writing everything that came to my mind.

Latina Hart, my sister, who kept saying, "Tell me another story."

My daughter, Seema Horman, who spent every minute she could just helping.

And my dad, Lee Roy Hart, who did not laugh when I wanted to see something outside the world given to me—he just showed me.

Thanks to all my family and friends who supported me.

And a special thanks to those at LongHorn Steakhouse #5469—without their help, my characters would have had no place to eat!

Thank you.

PART 1

Every Saint has a past, every Sinner has a future
—Oscar Wilde

CHAPTER 1

Mycheal sat at his desk and frowned at the scrolls in front of him.

This can't be right, he thought. He reread it. He checked the date. No, the date was correct. *How can this be? A human will resolve the war of souls nonviolently?*

Mycheal stared at the scrolls again. His mind began to wander, but it churned with more questions than answers. When would it all begin? Had it already? As he read on, he became more perplexed.

"A pure child of fire and earth shall be their guide," it said. Fire and earth? According to the laws, either you were a child of fire or a child of earth. Mixed blood was not considered pure. It was considered weak blood because it was more susceptible to dark angels and truly dark thoughts. The laws clearly stated that mixed blood could not resist their powers and could not be bound by the laws. Yet it specifically said that this child of mixed blood was pure. Could he and the Council of Arcs have been wrong?

Now he was left with the decision whether or not to share this information. Mycheal thought back to how he had come across the scrolls. What would the others think if they knew his secret?

Mycheal had always liked going to raves. He liked the music and energy of the very young. They seemed so carefree.

He had been raving in the Utah desert on a Native American reservation one day when he felt it—angelic energy. Not any energy, but the kind that was felt from his weapons. He followed the energy to a distant cave. The cave was quite difficult to get to. On the forefront. It look like it was a solid rock face. When Mycheal walked closer and saw that there was an opening. However, there was no immediate way of getting to it. He began to search around the base of the hill. Nothing. He glanced first to the left, then right to make sure no one was around to see what he was about to do. Mycheal released his wings. Unlike the myths, Angel wings are not White in color. His wings where 3 different shades of Blue ranging from a bright Navy Blue to shades of Teal. Once inside, Mycheal had found mounds of treasure and three scrolls. He took a closer look at the treasure. It look like someone just piled gold coins in five separate stacks. Then in the center was dishes made of gold and jewels, about a dozen of trunks filled with silk, a small arsenal of jeweled handled daggers and swords, sitting on the top, like a cherry, was the scrolls. The scrolls had been brimming with angelic energy. He'd carefully lifted the scrolls and flown toward the heavens with them.

How could he be certain that this was not a trick of the angels of darkness? He definitely could not figure this out without help. Besides, the more alone he was with the scrolls, the more paranoid he got. Mycheal brightened with an idea. He could trust his three best friends. Between the four of them, they could formulate a plan. He grinned. They hadn't been nicknamed the Four Horsemen for nothing!

Mycheal summoned a messenger and handed him three missives.

"Please wait for a response. They are rather important."

"Yes, sir." The messenger went off to complete his task.

Another messenger appeared, and a sweet voice called out, "An important missive, sir. It is First Echelon."

"Thank you. Is a response required?"

"No, sir."

"Leave it on the desk."

The messenger did as she was bade to do and left to deliver her other messages. Mycheal finished signing the documents he was working on and then reached for the missive. As he read it, he realized it was an unusual request—check that—order. Really, it was a very strong request. He sighed.

"I may as well get this over with," he said aloud and summoned his assistant, Zophael. Zophael appeared instantly. "Send for Xathaniel," Mycheal said. "Do not summon him. Send for him. It is the only way I can get him to take time off. Let him know he has a new assignment; otherwise, he will put it off for more important duties."

With a nod, Zophael left to carry out Mycheal's orders. Mycheal could feel the change coming. Ever since he had discovered the scrolls, he had felt the shift in the power source. Were the scrolls responsible? What did it all mean? Were others feeling it too?

Mycheal was so deep in his thoughts that he did not see or hear his best friends enter the office. It wasn't until Gabriel, always the practical joker, threw a paper airplane past Mycheal's face that he became aware.

"So, what's the story, chief?" Gabriel said with a cocky grin. When Mycheal gave him an annoyed look, Danjal, ever the peacemaker, slapped Gabriel on the back of the head.

"Pay no attention to this intelligent being; he has been reading Superman comics instead of catching up on text as he should."

"All work and no play will make me all moody and broody," said Gabriel. "But then again, I hear lady angels like the moody type. Right, moody boy?"

Gabriel turned his eyes to Rafayal. As often was the case, Rafayal ignored Gabriel's taunts and got straight to the point.

"We were all together when we received your missive. So we thought we'd save time and come straight away," Rafayal said. "Are you well?"

Mycheal nodded. "We need privacy for what we must discuss."

Gabriel's carefree demeanor instantly changed. In its place was the fearsome warrior of legend. "What is this all about?" he said.

Mycheal looked at each of them directly, hoping they would get his meaning. "Well, we have been really busy with our duties of late. How about we take a walk? Maybe to Hanna Lake? It would mean a couple of hours to ourselves. What do you say?"

Danjal was the first to jump up out of his seat. "Good idea. I could use a break. Hey, I have this problem I need to bounce off you, Myke. We can chat as we walk to the lake. You gentlemen don't mind, do you?"

"Mind? Us mind? I have no mind," Gabriel said. "Come on, moody boy. Let's tag along to keep things fun."

CHAPTER 2

Mycheal exited his office to find a crowd. That was nothing new. His duties included being chief of angels, the head of Leader Division of Angels (or LDA, as the angels referred to it), and the head of the Warrior Angel Division; he also served on the angel council. Recently, his office had been placed in charge of reassignments. It had come to the council's attention that some angels were getting bored or burned out with their assignments and were becoming targets for "nonservice" angels. These weren't angels of darkness, but they weren't angels in service either. Nonservice angels could be identified by the scarring, bruising, and/or sores found around their wrists and forearms. This was caused by the angelic script gauntlets worn by all angels. As the nonservice angels refused service, the gauntlets tightened, causing bruising and bleeding. The gauntlets could not be removed unless an angel was released from service. With the dark angels, the angelic gauntlets turned black and rotted away the skin. The Dark Angels somehow slowed the process.

Angels, nonservice angels, and dark angels. There were three sides, when there could only be two. And that was why there was another war. This time it was a civil war.

Mycheal made his way over to his assistant. Zophael had completed his earlier task and was back at his desk. No one was there at the moment. When Zophael looked up, Mycheal was standing there with Gabriel, Danjal, and Rafayal. Zophael stood up to greet them. As always, the privacy shield came up into place. The privacy shield allowed each angel to speak with confidence so no one else could hear what was being said during a session. Assignments remained just that—assignments. Council members felt it put less pressure on an angel if he or she had privacy when choosing to accept an assignment or not. Since its installation, 97 percent of angels had accepted their assignments; the rest had very good reasons for turning them down. Mycheal liked the gadget.

Before Zophael could utter a word, Mycheal patted his shoulder. "Is there anything urgent?"

"No, sir. Nothing I can't handle."

"What did we discuss about the *sir* thing? Hmm? Well, never mind. I need a break. I am going out for a while. Summon me the usual way if you need me."

Zophael watched Mycheal walk away, trailed by Gabriel making knock-knock jokes and Danjal welding a rubber toy hammer.

"If they're bad, I get to whack you, right?" Danjal said.

"Danjal, you come near me with that thing, and I'll put spiders in your armor for a week!" was heard as they sailed out the door.

Zophael laughed and shook his head. He only hoped that someday he would find a friendship as strong and loyal as the one that those four shared. They balanced one another. Friendships were important to angels. They lived for eternity, and companions were a wonder to have. Zophael thought of his two best friends, Azazel and Kadosh. The three of them had had different assignments, but they had always made time for each other. They had always done everything together. Then things began to shift, to change. First, Azazel started acting oddly. He started asking strange questions, such as, "Why should a son of fire be in service to a son of clay?" Then Kadosh began to question angelic service as well. Pretty soon, Zophael had nothing to talk to them about. He did not believe what Azazel believed, that the sons and daughters of Eve should be in service to sons of fire, and he did not believe, like Kadosh, that no service should be performed at all. So now, here he sat, helping when he could—and happy to do it. But he missed his friends.

Zophael was lost in thought, and when he raised his eyes, they clashed with Rafayal's dark ones. It was as if the other angel understood every feeling and thought that had passed through Zophael's mind. Zophael stood.

"May I help you, sir?"

"I know Mycheal's job is important. All of ours are, especially yours. Without you, he would be so overworked. But something has been bothering him of late."

"I thought it was my imagination—you know, me thinking too much. You noticed it too?"

"I think that this time to himself will help. If you can promise him a few hours, I can promise to have him back in time to address all the important issues you put off until then."

Zophael nodded, stunned. Rafayal hardly ever talked, and here he was, chatting with him like they were old friends.

"Then we are in agreement," Rafayal said.

Danjal's head appeared in the doorway of the crowded office. "Hey, Rafe! We're waiting on you."

Rafayal nodded at Danjal and walked toward the door. Other angels stepped to one side or another to allow him to pass. Halfway to the door, Rafayal stopped and turned to face Zophael. Zophael stood once again but remained behind his desk.

"Is there something else, sir?" he asked.

"*Sir* is no longer required, and secondly, I wanted to thank you." With that said, Rafayal turned and exited the room.

When Rafayal rejoined his friends, Mycheal asked, "What was that about?"

"Nothing much." Rafayal shrugged. Mycheal knew he wasn't going to get an answer from him.

"You know we can't go to the lake, right?" Rafayal said. "Too many people heard us say that that was where we were going."

Mycheal smiled. "I never intended to go there in the first place. Follow me. I have the perfect place."

Zophael stared at the empty doorway. Rafayal was now his friend. How did that happen? He shook himself and returned to work.

"Who is next, please?"

"Hello, my name is Echo."

Zophael looked up from his paperwork to see a caramel-colored angel with golden-brown eyes and black hair. He stood to greet his new guest.

"Hello, Echo. How may I help you today?"

"I am not sure if you can help me, but I was sent here. I hope you can assist me," she said. Her smile warmed his heart a bit.

"I promise to do my best."

"Well, I have never been to Earth, and you see, I am in charge of the children here."

Zophael gave her a puzzled smile. "Are you trying to say that you would like to be reassigned to the Watcher's Division?"

"No, no. I love my current assignment." Echo chewed nervously on her lower lip.

"Little sister, I am confused. You need to help me out a bit more."

"Okay, here goes. I would like to fall to Earth and live as a human for a time—just so I would know what it is like to be human."

"*What!?*" Zophael shook his head; he wasn't sure if it was in rejection or disbelief. "I am sorry. That is not a possibility. Wait, why do you want to do this?" His voice softened. "Is there … someone?"

Echo ignored his gentle probing. "Is the request rejected?"

Zophael straightened in his seat. "Not so much rejected as it is just not done. Besides, only First Echelon decides on those matters."

Echo got to her feet stiffly. Zophael rose and reached for her hand.

"I have a feeling there is more to this than you are sharing. I will not ask, but I will say that I am really sorry I was not able to help."

Echo smiled and shook his hand. "Thank you for trying," she said, and she turned and left.

He watched as she stopped to chat with a small group of angels. Sometimes he wished that he could do more. Mycheal made it all seem so easy.

"Okay. Next. Next angel, please."

The noise level in the room suddenly rose higher than normal. Zophael's eyes circled the room to determine the source. It wasn't long before the crowd parted to reveal Xathaniel in full battle gear. Xathaniel was third in command of the battle warriors, Danjal being the second and Mycheal being the first. Mycheal and Danjal had been blessed with other duties, but Xathaniel had the honor of assigning the warriors. Xathaniel's assignments came from Mycheal himself.

Xathaniel looked neither right nor left, making a beeline for Zophael's desk. Zophael remained standing until Xathaniel reached his desk.

Zophael motioned toward the chair, and with a smile and nod of thanks, Xathaniel sat down.

"I am sorry. I know there is a line," Xathaniel said.

"No need to worry. Mycheal will see you in a few hours. That gives you enough time to refresh yourself after your long journey."

"Thank you. I accept your offer. I shall return," Xathaniel said.

"Is there anything else I can do for you?" Zophael asked.

Xathaniel held out his hand. "No, thank you. You have been very helpful."

Zophael took Xathaniel's hand in a handshake. "You are welcome, sir."

Zophael thought he saw Xathaniel flinched as he called him *sir*, but he was sure he was mistaken. Maybe it was his imagination, after all, he had been working long hours as of late.

With that, Xathaniel exited, creating as much excitement as when he arrived. Zophael realized that Xathaniel walked through the crowd as if he did not hear what was being said about him, but Zophael could tell he heard every word.

How sad, he thought. *How would I react to speculation and gossip? Could it be so? Xathaniel do not like being the center of attention nor the hero worship.*

How did Zophael miss that? Maybe he did witness Xathaniel flinched when he called him sir. Hmm, there is more to him than he's projecting. Zophael had no time to muse over Xathaniel's problem just yet. He will come back to it, though.

As soon as Xathaniel left, another angel replaced him at Zophael's desk. The angel in question had tight, blond curls, blue eyes, and fair skin. He was how Earth picture books portrayed angels.

"So, what job did Xathaniel request? Is he not a battle warrior any longer?"

"Uh, what is your name, little brother?"

"Peter."

Zophael spoke to Peter as one would speak to a child. He had seen it before, one angel hero-worshipping another. He did not want to discourage the young angel's spirit, just give him knowledge so that he would not be recruited to the nonservice angels or to the angels of darkness.

"Well, Peter, you know as well as I do, as soon as an angel occupies that space where you are sitting, the privacy shield is in place. There is a reason for that. Confidence and upmost privacy. Now, little brother, what may I do for you?"

Zophael answer did nothing to dampen Peter's excitement.

"He's my hero! Wait until Timothy hears that I saw Xathaniel. You think I can work with him instead of the Harvest Division?"

"Peter, if you get assigned to the Battle Warrior Division, you have to go through training, and then there is no guarantee you will remain with battle warriors. You might be assigned with Pyriel of the Watcher's Division."

"You think if I stick around, Xathaniel will return?" Peter asked. "Don't you think he looked a little sad and tired?"

Peter craned his head to search the crowded room for the object of his hero worship.

"Peter!" Zophael did not mean to be sharp with the young angel. He sighed. "Are you paying attention to me?"

Peter faced Zophael. "Of course, sir. I want to be assigned to wherever Xathaniel goes—no matter where. I would be his assistant." Peter had a very determined look. He looked like a fierce battle angel.

Zophael had felt the same way when he met Mycheal. He had admired him, and he had wanted to learn all the things that Mycheal knew—the things he found so great about him. Once Zophael got over his awe, he realized how much work and pressure was on Mycheal, and all he wished to do was be a help to him. Zophael recognized the same things in Peter. Peter no longer looked like the angel in picture books. He resembled a protector.

"All right, Peter. If you are sure this is what you want, then we must talk. There is much to do. Return in a few hours."

Peter grinned. "Will I meet Xathaniel when I return?"

"Little brother, if all goes well, you will get your desired wish. Return in a few hours. There is much to be done."

Peter jerked up out of the chair and shot out of the office, followed by Zophael's hearty laugh and the curious stares of the remaining angels.

Now, this is what this job is all about, Zophael thought.

"Next angel, please."

CHAPTER 3

"I must admit, Myke: I would have never thought of this place," Gabriel said as he sat next to the stream.

"Agreed," said Rafayal. "Let's get down to business. I only got us a few hours of time from Zophael. He's a good find," he added, leaning against the nearest tree.

"It's more like he found me," Mycheal said and smiled at the memory.

"Why are we here?" Rafayal asked quietly.

Danjal plopped next to Mycheal on the ground. "Yes, what are we doing here? Not that I do not enjoy all of your company, but why could we not talk in your office?"

"For several reasons. I do not know about you, but I have what on Earth they call a leak. Someone is leaking information out. I know it is not Zophael, for he lost two friends—friends like you—because he believes in service and compassion."

"It could explain the problems I have been having of late." Gabriel's frown was unusual. "You have given me the final piece to a puzzle I have been working on. What about you, Rafayal? Have you noticed things that should not be happening?"

Rafayal nodded. "So our breach may be deep."

"Or shallow," Danjal countered. Three sets of eyes turned toward him.

"What do you mean?" Mycheal asked.

"Messengers. What if the information came from a handful of messengers?" As Danjal continued, he got more animated. "Think on it. Did we all put certain information in missives?" Danjal's eyes touched on each of his friends.

Rafayal was a strategist. It was what he was blessed with, and at that moment, Mycheal was grateful for it. "You may be right," Rafayal said. "There is a way to test this theory."

Mycheal gave a slow smile. "You have something, don't you?"

"Maybe. I need to observe a little more, but in the meantime, the simplest plan is the best."

"What do you have in mind? I hope it's sneaky," Gabriel said.

"Easy, Gabe. We'll get those responsible soon enough. Right now, we need to draw out the culprits. When we send out messages, we can use the codes we used as children," Rafayal said. "Remember?"

"Hey, remember me? I was not around then," Danjal protested.

"Oh, yeah—the baby!" Gabriel laughed.

Danjal stuck his tongue out at him as if to prove that point. "Stop giving me grief, and just tell me," he said.

Mycheal smiled. "It was rather childish and fun back then. When a word ended in *E,* we added the word *key* to the end, and then put our opposite meaning. If the word ended in *A,* we put *aye* at the end and, same as before, said just the opposite. *I* was *it, O* was *oat,* and *U* was *use,* and we always said the opposite of our meaning."

"The opposite was the fun part. It gave our teachers grief." Gabriel laughed.

Rafayal grinned. "A prankster from the start. Busted!"

Gabriel gave Rafayal a look of respect. "*Busted*? Looks like someone has been earthbound more than we thought."

Rafayal cocked his eyebrow at Gabriel but said nothing. Mycheal commanded the attention of his friends by clearing his throat. "Now we need to address another matter. And we have to discuss it here as I have no peace or quiet at my office."

"I know that feeling." Rafayal spoke as if his mind was elsewhere. He turned to find all eyes on him. "I am listening," he said.

"I do not know where to begin," Mycheal said and then sighed. "I have been sitting on a rather big secret."

"You mean the one where you go to raves?" Gabriel asked.

"*Gabriel!*" Danjal and Rafayal yelled in unison.

Mycheal looked stunned for a second and then laughed. "I should have known better, but that's not what I'm talking about." Mycheal was relieved that he no longer had to hide the secret of the raves. "What I'm talking about is my find."

"Find? What find?" Danjal asked.

"Three scrolls saturated with Angelic Energy."

"Start from the beginning." Gabriel said gravely.

Mycheal proceeded to tell them everything, including where he found the scrolls. When he finished, Mycheal added, "What puzzles me is the energy coming from them. Did any of you feel it? They were hidden in my office."

"No. I felt a change in you, though," Rafayal said.

"Is that what has been bothering you of late?" Danjal asked curiously. This time it was Rafayal's turn to look surprised. Rafayal, like many other angels, misjudged Danjal's wisdom and insight because of his age. The three angels waited for Mycheal's answer.

"Well, yes and no," Mycheal said and sighed.

"What is it? Yes or no? All kidding aside," Gabriel said earnestly, and added that he too had felt the change in Mycheal.

"Okay, everyone sit. Get comfortable. We have some issues to work through." Mycheal waited until everyone was seated before continuing. "If you feel me changing, I think I am. Let me explain. Ever since I found those scrolls, I have felt a shift in the power source. I'm constantly wondering if it's a trick from the dark angels. One of the passages from the scrolls states that the civil war of angels will cease nonviolently with a son of Adam or a daughter of Eve. Your thoughts?"

Mycheal looked at each of his friends expectantly. Gabriel was the first to speak. "You know, if this is a trick, it is expected for us to go on the defensive."

"You have an idea." Rafayal made a statement and not a question. It was clear to all what his friend was up to.

"Yeah …" said Gabriel slowly.

"Yeah, you see? Too many comic books." Danjal laughed.

"DJ, stop teasing Gabe," Mycheal said in annoyance. "We're running out of time. Go on, Gabe. We're listening."

"Now, what if we assign some watchers to this. But not just any watchers—ones with angel-warrior experience."

Mycheal could tell that Rafayal was rather impressed with Gabriel, but he also knew that he would not let the other angel know that just yet.

Rafayal weighed in. "With this assigned watcher's league, the watchers would all have to report to Mycheal and/or Danjal and no one else. Brilliant."

"How about if we form a small group for intel only," Danjal said. "We'll send an all-points missive saying we are investigating certain strange occurrences."

"Great, Danjal," Rafayal said. "And let's use our coded missive for that too."

"We will handle all problems as they come," Mycheal said. "No planning. Our meetings will be here, and we will use coded messages, always. If the missives are not coded, then something is amiss. Are we all in agreement?" he asked.

Rafayal nodded. "Agreed."

Danjal smiled. "Yes."

Gabriel slapped Mycheal on his back in a friendly manner. "I must admit, Mycheal, real genius picking the Garden of Eden as a meeting place."

"Yes, you said that already," Rafayal said. "Just agree to the terms, joke boy."

"Oh! Zinged by Rafe the Moody!"

"Just agree," Danjal said, laughing.

"I agree," Gabriel said. "Now, have any of you read *Superman, Man of Steel* comic?"

"Where's my toy hammer?"

"Ow! DJ! Quit it!"

CHAPTER 4

Mycheal returned to his office to find that Zophael had finish reassigning angels for the afternoon. He was glad. This was his favorite part of the day. The quiet allowed him to think and meditate. Sometimes he needed to get lost in his mind.

Mycheal was enjoying one of those sessions when he heard someone at his door. He pried one eye open to find Xathaniel standing quietly.

Mycheal laughed and got up to greet him. "And just how long were you planning on standing there?"

"Not long. I would have woken you up if need be." Xathaniel took Mycheal's hand in a firm handshake. "How are you, councilman?"

Mycheal winced at the title, but quick as a whip he fired back, "Very good, sir."

Xathaniel ducked his head in embarrassment. "Point well taken. Do you think I will ever get used to … I don't know, being addressed—"

"Like it is the be-all and end-all if we are displeased? Yeah, I'm not used to it myself." Mycheal indicated that Xathaniel should sit.

Xathaniel looked at his boss in surprise. "I would think that you would be used to the attention."

"Attention, yes. What follows, no," Mycheal said. "Still not used to the talk. You understand that there will always be talk—good, bad, or indifferent."

Xathaniel gave a bitter smile. "Duly noted. So why do I feel so alone at times? I feel like I can never spend time with my friends as you do. And worrying about who to trust sure makes it hard to develop new friendships." Xathaniel looked drained, sad, and tired after delivering that statement. "Seriously, Mycheal, how do you do it? How do you cope?"

Mycheal's smile was so bright that, for a moment, Xathaniel was worried. But he realized it was peace. Xathaniel want to envy such calm, but he did not have the heart for it. Mycheal deserved what he had earned.

"I have the blessing of Zophael," Mycheal said. "Without his assistance, I would be lost." He gave Xathaniel a soulful look. "Don't you think it's about time you find one who can assist you?" Mycheal gave a mischievous chuckle as he circled his desk to seat himself back behind it. "After all, you are few short steps from being an arc." Mycheal grabbed a slip of parchment and tossed it toward Xathaniel to view.

"*No!* This cannot be!" Xathaniel exclaimed as he examined the document. "Wait. It says I have one more assignment before I assume the position. Do you have any idea what it might be?"

Mycheal shook his head in the negative. "I am waiting for Zophael to bring it to me. He receives the assignments and arranges them. I do not dare touch his system. He will be here soon."

Xathaniel nodded his head in understanding. "So tell me, how is my old friend Danjal? Is he well?"

Mycheal laughed. "Ah, he has taken up hanging around with Gabriel. At first it concerned me."

"And now?"

"Now, it does not. Danjal has the gift of keeping everyone's heart pure. It is what is needed in these times. Subject change—is Avial still beside you at every given turn?"

Xathaniel gave a hearty laugh. "Of course. Where else would he be? I guarantee he is here somewhere close by."

"Why do you not call him to be your assistant? Would it not solve your … situation?"

As quick as the smile had come to Xathaniel, it vanished.

"No," he said. Mycheal gave him a puzzled look. At the look, Xathaniel continued. "I am ashamed to admit it, but I am not sure if Avial's feelings toward me are born of gratitude, of hero worship, or of intense loyalty."

"What is wrong with that?" Mycheal asked. "When Zophael arrived, he had a case of hero worship."

"I do not know. I cannot say. Just a feeling I have. Make no mistake, Avial is as honorable and trustworthy as you can get."

Mycheal waited patiently for Xathaniel to talk out the issues. He was used to counseling the angels that sat in his office. It did not matter if Mycheal was disciplining them or just plain listening—he knew that sometimes it helped just to vent.

"Avial is the best friend and lieutenant I could ever hope for," Xathaniel said.

"But," Mycheal prompted.

"It is when he reminds me of the life debt that I become unsure of the friendship. Is he my friend because I saved him or in spite of it?"

"Would your feelings for him change?"

Xathaniel looked indignant. "Of course not!"

"Then, my friend, you are creating a problem that does not exist. Besides, I do not think Avial will be suited to be your assistant as an arc."

"Well, it is a good thing we have a long wait before I become an arc, right?"

Mycheal remained silent with an amused *Yeah, right* look on his face.

"No, no, no! This cannot be happening! *When?!*" Xathaniel now had a look of pure panic on his face.

Mycheal would have teased and laughed at him, but he could see his genuine distress. He put on his "serious boss" face. The latest missive was very clear. Xathaniel had one last assignment to perform, and then he would be given a blessing as an arc.

"One assignment away. My advice to you, Xathaniel, is to prepare yourself. You will have a space on the Council of Angels as well."

"Please tell me you are kidding, sir."

Mycheal looked Xathaniel in the eye. "No. I am to be your mentor." Mycheal got up from behind his desk, came around the front, and sat on the edge in front of Xathaniel. "It is time. You cannot hide your light forever. I have faith that you can do this."

Xathaniel nodded his consent.

"You understand you have to speak the binding words to relight your service gauntlets," Mycheal said.

"Yes, sir. I understand."

"Good. I will give Zophael a little more time, and you may tell me how you spent your free time today."

Zophael gave the young angel, Peter, a harsh look. "Pay attention! Do you remember everything I taught you today?"

"Yes. But I am confused. Am I to stay here while he goes on his mission?"

"You are to go wherever you are required. You are training to assist an arc, and it is no easy task."

Zophael continued. "Now, are you ready? We are going to meet Mycheal to present Xathaniel with the details of his new assignment. Remember—you are to address them both as *sir* unless otherwise specified. Any questions?"

"No. Let us proceed."

At that moment, Zophael could find no trace of the young angel that had tried his patience for most of the day. When they began, Peter had spent the first part of the training quoting everything he ever heard about Xathaniel, his hero. Zophael had to explain to him that being an assistant to an arc was quite different from what he might have imagined. Zophael would have liked to warn him of the trials, but he felt it would be best if Peter experienced them himself and adjusted as needed. All he could do was to offer Peter the tools he would need to complete his task. Zophael sighed. *Yes, Mycheal does make this all look easy.*

Both angels proceeded to make their way to Mycheal's office. All was quiet, as expected. Upon their arrival, Zophael was very much surprised to find Avial sitting by the door leading to Mycheal's inner office. He was dressed in full battle gear, waiting patiently.

"Peace be with you, Brother," Zophael greeted.

"And with you, little brother." Avial stood and embraced Zophael in a bear hug. "You are well?"

Zophael's smile was bright. "I am well. What are you doing here?"

"I came with Xathaniel." He offered no other explanation. In truth, Zophael did not expect one. "Who is this?"

"Oh, forgive my rudeness. Avial, might I present Peter? He is your general's new assist."

"Greetings, little brother. Peace be with you."

"Greetings, sir. Peace be with you as well."

Avial frowned. "Wait. Is it happening now?"

Zophael's face voided of all expression. "I have no idea of which you speak," he said.

Avial burst out laughing. "You have not changed, my friend. Of course, you cannot discuss the matter. I knew it was going to happen. He denies it."

"So, you are not offended that you were not chosen as his assist?"

"No. I would be bad at it. I have no patience to be diplomatic. I am a warrior through and through. When Xathaniel is appointed, I shall humbly offer myself as his personal guardian."

Peter, who had been unusually quiet throughout the conversation, spoke up. "It would be my honor to accept your name to be in service of my angel arc, Xathaniel."

Perfect, Zophael thought. *Executed perfectly. Posture and respect, and he spoke the binding words with dignity.* Zophael smiled. Peter was going to serve Xathaniel well. Now to find a second for Avial. Little did his friend know, he would be the next leader for the Watcher's Division. Zophael glanced up in time to see Peter at Zophael's desk with Avial. They were talking quite animatedly. Zophael could not hear what they were discussing because the privacy shield was in place. He watched as Peter pushed a document toward Avial for his signature. Avial signed, and as soon as his signature was complete, new markings became visible on his service gauntlets. The new marks were different from the ones he had had. Zophael noticed the marks were golden in color, and they were glowing. For a moment, the ground shifted under him, and his angelic power stirred. What was that?! He came back to himself when he heard Avial give a rich chuckle. "Little brother, you are going to have you hands full with my general. He has a rigid sense of duty when it comes to others, but none when it comes to his safety. Good luck!"

"Did you guys feel that?" Zophael asked excitedly. Both set of eyes returned his stare with puzzlement.

Zophael glanced from one to another. He decided that they were not jesting for his benefit. "I guess it was nothing. I just need rest. I have been working rather hard of late."

Before either angel could respond, Mycheal's voice boomed as he walked out of his office. "Zophael, we have been waiting."

"Sorry, sir. We have been tending to the business of the appointment of Xathaniel."

"Good, good. Then I will see all three of you in here now." Mycheal turned back toward his office. Avial and Peter trailed behind him.

Zophael took a critical look around and then scooped up the necessary paperwork to follow. He paused halfway to his destination.

"What was that?" he asked out loud to no one in particular.

"Still waiting!"

"Yes, sir. On my way." Zophael sailed in Mycheal's office to perform his duty.

CHAPTER 5

Xathaniel looked out at the city from his rooftop perch. It was a little after nine o'clock at night, and Avial was late.

"I am not late. I got here in time to check out this location to make sure of its safety," Avial said.

Xathaniel chuckled. "Always watching my back, right?"

"Your back, front, and side. It is what I do," said Avial.

Xathaniel turned to greet his friend. In the three months that he had been assigned to this apartment building, it had not been attacked—nor had any other angel been there except Avial. When he received new orders to watch a woman in the building, instead of the building itself as originally ordered, his assignment became more puzzling.

Xathaniel could feel a shift in the power source, but he could not explain it.

He greeted Avial. "Hello, my friend. What news?"

Avial looked at his general and friend closely. Xathaniel had been distracted as of late. When he had told Avial that he had been reassigned, Avial's heart lightened. It was a chance for Xathaniel to leave his duties to others for a time.

Avial felt a slight shift in the power source. Could he be mistaken? It only happened once, so he could not be sure.

It was no secret that Xathaniel would soon be appointed an archangel, arc, for short but the angel denied it. Personally, Avial thought it was because he hated hero worshiping among the angels. Avial had watched as Xathaniel walked among the warrior angels, and he listened to the talk. Xathaniel said that he didn't know if the others were friends or if they were there just because of his name. He considered Avial and Danjal as his only true friends. Xathaniel had lost his entire family to dark angels, so he had no one else close to him. He had devoted his life to bringing justice for any being—human and angel alike—who had lost loved ones to darkness. What could you say to someone like that? Just being there for him was good enough for Xathaniel—it was not good enough for Avial though.

Avial did not like to see his friend so full of worry and confusion. He would give it a few more days and then address it with him. Avial looked up and saw Xathaniel watching him expectantly.

"No one has been assigned to your post," Avial said.

"That's odd. It's been three and a half months," Xathaniel said.

"Then it must be true," Avial replied.

"What?" Xathaniel asked.

Avial debated whether to share all the rumors and speculations; after all, they were often more trouble than they were worth. Rumors had hurt his friend more times than he wanted to remember. He had been Xathaniel's right hand for many years, always watching his flank—not that he needed it. But Xathaniel had saved him from becoming a dark angel, and for that, Avial would be forever grateful.

Xathaniel's ice-blue eyes clashed with Avial's golden-brown ones.

"Stop stalling, Avial. You would think that, after all these years, you would know that I know when you do not want to tell me something. Spit it out!"

"*Spit it out*?!"

"Yes," Xathaniel said. "I've learned a few expressions since coming here." His expression lit up. "They are so ... different. They sometimes describe exactly what I'm feeling. And the food! Wow! So many textures and tastes."

Avial smiled. This was the friend he missed: always a warrior but with the heart and excitement of a child when introduced to something new.

"Well, what I know and what I feel are two different things," Avial said.

"Tell me all, rumor or otherwise. You said no one has been appointed or assigned to my post, correct?" Xathaniel said.

"True. About three months ago, they started reassigning watchers and battle angels. Do you think we are preparing for battle?"

Xathaniel gave it some deep thought. "Yes, but not the kind we are used to. Tell me everything, fact and rumor."

"I've told you everything that is a fact, except about the all-points missives with the strange words. But I think they are just mistakes being made by Zophael. I think something is happening here on Earth."

"Yes. I got that impression as well when I was assigned a building, which is now a woman. Another strange occurrence. Please continue."

"Now, to rumor. Rumor has it that Mycheal needs some time off, so he formed an elite squad to keep an eye on things."

"Once again, odd. That does not sound like Mycheal. First Zophael, now Mycheal. It does not add up."

"I think that is why you were assigned here."

Xathaniel sighed. "We can play guessing games all decade long, however nothing will be revealed until it is time."

"Very true, my friend. So, tell me about the things you have discovered here." Avial laughed. "I wager there are many more wonders."

"Yes, there are. Pizza! Pizza is one of them. You can put just about anything on pizza."

"Really? Do tell me everything."

"Like chicken, beef, pineapple—mmm. It is delicious!"

Avial laughed a big hearty laugh. He was enjoying his friend's behavior.

"Corned beef, Dijon mustard, rye bread, *and* coconut cake!"

"I presume all of this is food." Avial smiled with a lift of his eyebrow.

"Yes. And there is this thing called gaming. Talk about fun! Oh, and I went bowling for the first time yesterday and—" Xathaniel suddenly stop talking.

"What is wrong?"

"Shhhh." Xathaniel cocked his head to one side. "She's awake."

"Who is awake?"

Xathaniel gave Avial a look like he had two heads. "The one I am assigned to."

"You can feel her? What does it mean?"

Xathaniel did not pretend not to understand his question. "Nothing. I never questioned it. I thought it was gifted to me with my new assignment."

"Now, it's my turn to say it: that's odd."

"That's right—you were a watcher at one point. So this is not normal?" Xathaniel asked.

"It is a blessing, my friend. If you were sent to watch her, you can track her as well if she is in trouble." A look of sadness passed between them both.

"Think no more of it, Avial."

"I try. But every once in a while …"

Xathaniel nodded. "I understand. I have to go. Peace be with you, Brother."

"As with you."

CHAPTER 6

He is here again. She could feel it. He didn't talk very much. He had said maybe four words in two or three months, but Kemia Reid knew when he was there. She didn't know how she knew he was male though. She never gave a thought to how she connected to this being or why he did not frighten her. She refused to give in to such nonsense. There were many things in the world that could not be explained, and it was not her job to explain them.

Kemia was tired. She was tired of fake friends and fake family alike—not knowing what to say to her, just waiting for her to die to see who would get her money. She was tired of tests. She was tired of doctors. She was tired of hospitals, and most of all, she was tired of dying. The doctors had informed her, very diplomatically, that there was nothing they could do but make her comfortable—although they said they would not give up. But how can you be comfortable leaving everything you know?

"Don't give up," her invisible male friend buzzed.

Kemia couldn't help answering. "Why shouldn't I? Look around; there's no one here. Why do you suppose that is? Bravery only last so long."

"You have to find those answers yourself. And as for bravery, it lurks in the shadows, making itself known when it is needed." He chuckled. "Besides, you're an adventurer. Think of this as an adventure."

"I do adore going on my adventures. Maybe that is why it was so hard to give up my career as a professional photographer. I do love to travel." She thought wistfully, *Maybe that's why I never found my other half. Ah well, too late for that now.*

A knock sounded on the door, and it was immediately opened by a pretty nurse. "Ms. Reid, do you need anything?"

"No, thank you."

As Kemia answered her, the nurse was looking inside the closet and bathroom.

"Are you okay?" Kemia inquired.

The nurse looked puzzled. "Um, yeah. Sure. Do you have a guest?"

"No. You know I never have guests. Why?"

"I could have sworn I heard you talking to someone."

"I was watching TV. It was keeping me company." She indicated the blank set. "I was talking back at a show. I finally got disgusted and turned it off!"

With a laugh, the nurse wrote something in Kemia's chart. "That explains it. Some of the shows I watch aren't that great either, but they are all that's on when I get home, and I'm too tired for much of anything else. I'll see you tomorrow night. They switched me to the late shift."

"Thanks for checking on me. Enjoy your time off."

"You're welcome. Well, I'm off to enjoy a terrible relationship." With a wave, the nurse left.

Kemia waited. He was still there. After ten minutes, she got annoyed.

"I know you're there," she said out loud. "Show yourself! I'm real tired of all this. You have been hanging around for three months. *Enough!*"

Xathaniel was stunned. She had known about him all along. He debated about making his presence known. It was against the rules for an angel to show his or her presence unless permission was obtained and/or it was a part of an assignment. But did it change things if she already knew? He decided that he would not be breaking any rules by making himself visible.

Xathaniel complied with her request. He made himself visible to her for the very first time.

What Kemia saw appear before her was a man wearing jeans, a T-shirt, boots, and a long coat. He was at least six feet tall with beautiful blue eyes and very dark hair cut in a military style.

"Greetings, Ms. Kemia Reid. My name is Xathaniel." He bowed formally.

"You know my name?"

"Of course. I've been assigned to you."

"Assigned? Exactly who are you?"

Xathaniel leaned in closer toward her. "Can you keep a secret?"

"I keep many secrets."

He gave a wicked grin. "Good, so can I."

Kemia laughed. "Okay, keep your secret. Why have you been with me for three months? Is that a part of your secret?"

"Actually, the secret is a secret no more. I've been assigned as your angel."

"My angel? I see. Waiting for me to pass, right? Well, stick around. My doctors only give me a few weeks."

"I know. I felt your anger and sadness."

"I'm not angry because I'm dying. I was angry at you."

"Me?" Xathaniel had had many emotions hurled at him, envy, jealousy, and even fear, but never anger. Frankly, he was quite surprised. "Why?"

"There's nothing as frustrating as being stalked by an angel. Who will I call? The heavenly cops? I can hear it now, 'Yes, Your Honor, he was in my apartment but didn't do anything or take anything.' Oh, yeah, loony bin for sure." Kemia laughed.

"I have questions."

"Good. I have some for you too. Mind keeping me company for a while?"

Xathaniel was more than happy to chat with Kemia. He finally had someone to talk to without an agenda. His friend Avial had been saved by him, so sometimes he didn't know if he was listening to Xathaniel out of obligation. Then there was Danjal. Danjal the compassionate, friends with all he encountered. And Mycheal. Mycheal was the leader of all angels. It was his duty to listen to angels.

"It would be my honor, my Lady Kemia." Xathaniel bowed.

"Okay, what's with the bowing stuff and calling me Lady?"

"Last question first. Lady is your title of respect. And I bow to you as I am at your service."

"You are rather sweet. If there is anything I can do for you, I am at your service. See? That's what friends are for. Is that a song?"

Xathaniel looked puzzled. Kemia laughed. "Sorry," she continued, "bad joke. Your turn, what are your questions?"

"I have only three. First, what is a loony bin? Is it a holder of some kind? Second, who is this "my honor"? And last, how did you know about my presence for the last three months?"

Kemia smiled at Xathaniel. "Are you serious? Haven't you been here before?"

"No, this is my first earthly assignment."

"Well, if I weren't so sick, I would show you the wonders." Kemia brightened. "Hey, have you had a cheeseburger yet?"

Xathaniel's eyes lit up with interest. "Is that food?"

She giggled. "Of course."

He sighed. "I must admit, here you have so many different things to eat. Food tasting is becoming my hobby."

"What if you run out of food?" Kemia laughed. "What will be your new hobby?"

After a moment's thought, Xathaniel realized that Kemia was teasing, something else new. No one has ever teased him before. He had done it, and he had been taken at face value, so he had to stop. With Kemia, he somehow knew she would just tease him back.

"Impossible! You can never run out. All you have to do is combine one food with another, and there! Another food to taste!"

Kemia thought he resembled a child on a new discovery. *Too bad I'm sick,* she mused. *I would love to take him to one of my favorite restaurants—just to see his face and eyes as he discovered the menu.*

"I feel your sadness again," Xathaniel said.

"Believe it or not, it's for you," she said.

"Me? My Lady, you have nothing to feel sad about when it comes to me."

She knew that he could still feel how sad she was. To take her mind off of her sadness, she decided to educate him on Earth stuff.

"Stop stalling," he said. "Answer my questions. I need to know about food next."

Kemia laughed out loud. "Bossy much? Okay, easiest question first. It's not *my honor;* it's *Your Honor.* It's a title giving to a judge—one who makes rulings in a court of law. Next, a loony bin is a hospital for the mentally sick. And last, I don't know how I knew you were there—I just did. I have always been different, ever since childhood."

Suddenly, Kemia felt an overwhelming bout of sadness and queasiness all at once. At the same time, Xathaniel grabbed his chest as if he couldn't breathe. He started to collapse.

"Nate? *Xathaniel!* Who do I call for help? What is your best friend's name?"

"Avial," he croaked out.

Kemia thought with all her might, *Avial, whoever you are, where ever you are, please help my friend! He's in trouble!*

Xathaniel began to fall to the floor.

An instant later, as Xathaniel's shoulders were about to touch to the floor, Avial caught him and wrapped his arms around his waist.

"I've got you, my friend."

They both heard Kemia say weakly, "Leave them alone, you jerk!"

"Are you visible, Avial?"

"Of course not. It is against the rules."

As the pain eased, Xathaniel thought to warn his friend. Before he could get a chance, Kemia said, "You're both safe now. Whoever you are, I thank you for helping my friend Xathaniel. He's special to me."

Avial had a look of mild surprise. "Of course, for his is my friend as well. I owe him my life, although he has refused it."

Kemia smiled. "Yup, sounds just like my friend. I think I'll keep him."

Avial laughed heartily. "Do you share?"

"Of course. Are you going to show yourself or are you more comfortable invisible?"

Avial looked at Xathaniel for guidance; it was very clear that he was not going to get any. Avial made himself visible. Kemia found herself looking at a man dressed in jeans, tennis shoes, and a nice pullover. He wore a lightweight jacket. He was five foot eight, with a stocky build, dark blond hair, and soft, golden-brown eyes.

"You had darker hair when I was a child," she said. "Did you dye it? And your eyes were steel gray." Kemia smiled warmly. "Nice to see you again, Arvial."

Both angels stood staring at Kemia Reid in stunned silence.

"Did I say your name wrong?" she asked.

Avial came out of his trance. "Arvial is not my name, my Lady Kemia. Avial, at your service." He bowed formally. "You have met my brother. Might I inquire when?"

"When I was a child of maybe six or seven. I was at an orphanage. It was really a group home, but none of us had parents."

Xathaniel took one of Kemia's hands into his. He didn't question his actions, it seemed natural. Somehow, he felt he had known Kemia forever, instead of a few hours. Kemia's reaction to his touch was to simply smile. She seem to share his feelings. "Would you be so kind as to tell us the story, Lady? That is, if it is not too painful to you." They were staring into each other's eyes.

For a moment, Avial thought they had forgotten that he was there, and then Kemia turned and addressed him. "Is Arvial well? Nothing's bad has happen to him, has it?"

"My brother is well. Please tell us the story, and I, no, we, will give you any information you would like to know, if it is in our power."

"I am at your service, Mr. Avial and Mr. Xathaniel—title of respect," she said with a nod. "Now, where to begin? Like I said, I was in a group home, and I was the youngest by two years; it stood to reason that no one wanted to play with me. It was well known that I created worlds of my own. I wasn't in school as of yet, so I did not have friends. Anyway, one day, I was playing in my fort in the backyard. The woman that ran the place, who we called Grandmother, was trying to get me to come inside to eat lunch, but I was having too much fun in my fort. It was then that I saw your brother stumbling past the fence line; he was being chased by some weird shadows—yucky things." She shuddered in memory. At her pause, Kemia went into a coughing fit. Xathaniel handed her a tissue. When she removed it from in front of her mouth to throw away, it was stained with bright red blood. Xathaniel next handed her a glass of water. After a few minutes, Kemia's body was calm.

Avial sat down at the bottom of the bed and tapped her foot lightly. "Go on," he encouraged.

"I jumped from my fort and ran over to him and took his hand. I asked if he was all right. He smiled and said he needed a friend. I told him I would be his friend. He said he didn't have much time. And then the yucky things tried to eat him. I stood up and told the shadows to go away, to stop hurting my friend. I remember wishing with all my might that Arvial would not be hurt. The next thing I knew, I felt arms lift me up in a hug. I opened my eyes, and Arvial introduced himself. He said his life was mine, and he was in my debt. Of course, I didn't know what that meant, so I asked. He just smiled and said that all I had to do was ask him for something, and he would do his best to give it to me. I asked for friends. He said he would do his best, but he asked if I would settle for a brother instead. I was overjoyed. I had family at last."

An overwhelming wave of sadness blanketed the room. Both angels felt it weigh them down.

Xathaniel stroked Kemia's hair and whispered, "Be easy, Lady. We are here for you. Tell us the rest."

Tears were leaking silently from Kemia's eyes. She continued, "One day, it had to be almost two years later, Arvial came to me in the middle of the night. He told me he had to go away, and he didn't know if he would ever come back. He said he hated leaving his little sister, but there were others who needed his help, and if he did not give it to them, the yucky shadow things would get them. Arvial wanted me to be the bravest sister in the world because I was the only one he had left. We were both crying. He kissed me on my forehead and left. I was crying so hard that I woke the kids that I shared my room with. Grandmother told me I was dreaming and needed friends. The following week she got me into this art club. I was really into taking pictures. I thought I met a true friend there, and I told him the story of my 'big brother.'" Kemia sobbed. "He betrayed me. The next thing I knew I was asked to leave to the club. After all, it was no place for 'special children.' I really thought I had dreamt it all until I saw you." Kemia faced Avial. "Are you and your brother twins?"

"No, Lady Kemia. I am older."

"When I was younger, I saw others like you, but I was unaware that you were invisible until that day at the art center. Grandmother said that everyone had invisible friends until they made real ones. Sure enough, I had my first sleepover one month later, and I never saw or heard you guys again until three months ago." She looked up and found the two angels smiling at her.

Xathaniel was the first to speak. "See? Brave."

"Oh, stop bragging."

"Who, me?" Xathaniel teased.

Kemia laughed. "Yeah, the know-it-all."

Avial watched his friend tease Kemia and her tease him back. He had never seen Xathaniel react that way. "Lady, I have questions," Avial said.

"I will answer them—*if* you stop calling me Lady."

"What may I call you?"

"Kemia is fine. After all, it is my name."

Avial glanced at Xathaniel and gave him a mischievous grin. "As you wish, little sister."

"Better. What is it you need to know?"

"Have you seen these shadow creatures since your childhood?"

"No. Is that what they are called? What aren't you telling me?"

"There is more going on than we know." Avial started to say more. He tipped his head slightly. "I am being summoned. I must go." He stood and bowed formally toward Kemia. "Peace be with you, my newfound little sister. I will petition for your life."

Xathaniel got up and walked over to his friend and placed a gentle hand on his shoulder. "Are you sure? Do you know what you are doing? It is a dangerous task."

Avial nodded. "I am, and if my brother becomes aware of what I am doing, he will surely take my side."

"Then go. Tell him. You have my petition as well. Peace be with you, my friend."

"As with you." They clasped hands in friendship before Avial disappeared.

Xathaniel stared out the window. He realized it was the first time that he did not question Avial's motive of friendship. It felt like a weight had been lifted off his chest. He felt light, free. How had that happened? He shook his head to clear it. Questions would be answered at the right time and not before, he had learned.

CHAPTER 7

Kemia had watched both men talk in low voices until Avial disappeared. Xathaniel continued to stare out the window. After five minutes of silence, Kemia couldn't take it anymore.

"Is he coming back?"

Xathaniel turned to face Kemia. She noticed he had a far-off look in his eyes. Whatever they had been talking about must have been serious.

"Maybe. I do not know. He was being summoned."

"What did he mean, that he will petition for my life?"

"It is hard to explain, but I will try." Xathaniel made his way to her bed and stood at the end.

"If I don't understand something, I will ask, so forgive my dumb questions ahead of time."

"Ask whatever you wish, Lady Fire."

"A new nickname. Cool!"

"Only I get to call you Lady Fire though. Is that permissible?"

"Of course, but only if I get to call you a name that only I can call you. Agreed?"

"We are in agreement." Xathaniel sat on the bed and took Kemia's hand and kissed it old-world style. "What will be my name?"

"I don't know. I haven't thought of it yet. Tell me about the petition, please."

"You are very sick, and your life force is ebbing away. This you know already. What Avial is petitioning for is a healing or a place in heaven."

"Wait. Please explain the difference."

"With a healing, you would live your life to your late '90s and get nothing more than a common cold. When you pass on, your soul will go to the hall of souls and will be reborn again and sent back to Earth. With the other, he will be petitioning for you to have a permanent home in heaven."

"Are you telling me that when we die we don't go to heaven?"

"Of course you go to heaven. But you don't stay there. You stay until you are recalled back to Earth. It could be as few as five years or as long as twenty years. Twenty years is the longest I've seen."

"I think I've got it, but there's a piece missing. Why can't everyone stay in heaven and not be reborn?"

"People make mistakes, so they are sent back to correct those mistakes."

Kemia stared at Xathaniel with wide eyes. "How many times does a soul have to be reborn to Earth?!"

Sadness entered his eyes. "Some give up the desire of man and allow the dark shadows to control their minds. Most people are weak with one kind of addiction or another."

"You mean like recreational drugs or alcohol?"

"Yes, and more—and maybe not those, but other things."

"Like what?"

"Vanity, power, money, sex—things like that."

"I understand. Please don't be sad. Finish telling me about the petition." She squeezed his hand in comfort. "Now, tell me—why would I not be put in this hall of reborn souls?"

"Because, Lady Fire, you have come to the aid of two warrior angels."

"Didn't Avial chase those things off earlier?"

"No, Fire, you did."

"I did? How?"

"You really have no idea of your gift, do you? No need to worry; we will figure it out. Why were you sad when I first was assigned to you?" Xathaniel asked.

"Forget it. It's been gloomy enough around here for one night. Tell you what—I'll share my happiest memory."

"No, please tell me about that day. For some reason, it still bothers you. It bothers me as well. You try to hide it, but I feel everything." Xathaniel looked deeply into Kemia's eyes. "Please? You were crying that day. You have not since."

Kemia sighed. "I went to my family to tell them about my illness. I wanted to be encircled with love and support. Instead, I found out I was adopted for a trust fund. When I lived in the group home, no one told me I had a trust fund. I truly loved my adopted parents. There is nothing like finding out that your family has been nice to you only because you kept them in the lifestyle they wanted. My adopted sisters are away at private schools, so they have no idea I am sick, and my parents will not tell me where they are. After all, they are their natural children; why should I have contact?" Kemia said bitterly. "And so now," she continued, "I have to go through this alone."

Xathaniel gave their linked hands a squeeze. "You are not alone. I am a little puzzled though. How did you find out they adopted you for the money? And how did they find out about the trust fund?"

"My adopted father was a paralegal at a law firm handling trusts and estates. When that lawyer died, he was asked to get all the case files organized for another attorney to take over. My file was among them. I was the only client that was a ward of the state by that time; everyone else had actual family to look after their interests. I'm not sure why I had a private attorney if I was a ward of the state. The day I came to the house to tell them about my illness, I heard them arguing about whether or not I had a will and how they were going to get legal help to obtain the rest of my money. You see, when I graduated college, I invested my trust. But I first gave my adopted parents one quarter of it, thinking that I was helping people who loved me."

"What did you do after you heard them?"

"They were in the kitchen, and I had started to enter the room when I heard them. I snuck back to the living room and then made a big production of coming to the kitchen. After a few minutes, I said that I couldn't stay, and I left. The rest is history."

"I was assigned to you shortly after?"

"Try ten minutes after. Well, you know me. I had a short pity party, and then I went to my attorney's and drew up a proper ironclad will."

"Do you think your parents will be surprised with the results?"

Kemia roared with laughter. "They will pass out."

Xathaniel face was marred with worry. "I just thought of something."

"What?"

"If I can feel you, dark angels can as well. That explains the shadow seekers."

"Is that what those things are called? Not to sound dumb, but so what? If I can get rid of them, no harm, no foul."

"You do not understand. Shadow seekers stay to the shadows to collect information to give back to the dark angels. My guess is that you are too powerful for them to come near right now, but they are gathering intel. I have the same powers that they do. The seeker attacked me; you tried to kill the seeker and succeeded but weakened me in the process. This is only a guess. You are something new."

"So, let me see if I can understand this," Kemia said. "You have been sent to look after me, for an unknown reason. Upon arriving, you discovered I have some sort of power against demons, but because it's different somehow, it weakens angels too."

"Yes."

"Now tell me, why me? How did this happen?"

"My Fire, I wish that I could give you answers, however, I cannot. For I do not have them myself," he said solemnly.

"This is not a tragedy, Xathaniel, just a mystery."

"Or a blessing. It depends on how you view it," Xathaniel said.

"Blessing? Oh, you mean my power."

"That too. Humans tend to destroy or overuse things of such nature. It is best to limit contact." Kemia looked at him, puzzled. "That is why your life force is ebbing away at such a young age," he said.

"I see. What does the petition entail? Will you and Avial get in trouble because of me? You're now my friends; I don't want to lose you too." She yawned.

Xathaniel stood and covered Kemia with a blanket. "Rest, Lady Fire. I shall lay watch."

"I meant to ask you, why do you call me Lady Fire?"

Xathaniel smiled as Kemia yawned again. "You are Lady Fire because your mind, spirit, and soul always burn bright. It does not matter if it is kindness, love, or anger—it burns."

"Those are the most beautiful words I have ever heard. I don't feel like I am all those things. Is that why you will petition for me? The fire thing?"

He laughed and kissed her on the forehead gently. "No. Enough questions for the night. Sleep. You have learned much today."

"Xathaniel, don't leave me, okay? I will be lonely without you."

"I will not go unless I have to," he promised. "Rest easy, my Fire."

Xathaniel walked over to the window. Kemia's hospital room was on the eighth floor, so he could see the city view. He liked the twinkling lights. He turned his sights skyward. Xathaniel couldn't see the stars, but he knew they were there. He closed his eyes in silent prayer. *Father, I am grateful for another day to be in service to you. I know I am being tested. I do not expect an answer. We in your service are always being tested and pushed. Many things puzzle me.*

Love washed over Xathaniel and a gentle, but strong voice in his head said, *Xathaniel, my child, what troubles you?*

Strange things are happening; are they of the dark realm? He did not have the heart to ask if Kemia's powers were dark. If they were, it would put a hole in his heart that he was not ready to face.

Be easy, young warrior; all is as should be. If you are in need, look to the four. Quick pictures of Mycheal, Danjal, Gabriel, and Rafayal flashed behind his eyes.

Thank you for your everlasting love and wisdom. Amen.

When Xathaniel opened his eyes, he felt all the tension leave his body instantly. He felt better. Then he was puzzled. Why not just Mycheal? After all, Mycheal was his leader. The Four Horsemen? This must be serious. Xathaniel felt the floor beneath his feet shift, and at the same time a wave of dizziness assaulted his senses. Another shift in the power source! This was the second time he felt it. More questions with even fewer answers.

Peace be with you, my brave warrior.

Xathaniel smiled. *I will be brave. Peace be with you.*

CHAPTER 8

As the early morning light stretched its fingers slowly over the city, light erasing dark, Xathaniel felt an angelic presence. He turned to find Rafayal standing quietly behind him.

"Xathaniel," Rafayal greeted.

"Rafayal. Is there something amiss?"

"I was summoned to perform a duty," Rafayal said.

"Good morning, Xathaniel," Kemia said from her hospital bed. "Who's your friend?"

Rafayal looked at Xathaniel. "I am not visible. This cannot be," he said.

"She can hear you as well," Xathaniel said and laughed.

Kemia yawned. "I'm going to pretend I don't hear you two. La, la, la …"

"Lady, stop teasing. He has come to visit you. Alas, we must conduct some business first."

"Well, if you gentlemen will excuse me." Kemia made her way to the bathroom and closed the door firmly.

As soon as she closed the door, Rafayal spoke. "Kemia Reid can see and hear us. Has this always been so?"

"According to her, yes."

"If I did not bear witness to this, I would not believe it. Then again …"

"She saved me from seekers."

"Yes. Avial reported it."

"Has he petitioned yet? I warned him of the danger. The shadow seekers are becoming more powerful than they have been in the past."

Rafayal nodded. "He has petitioned your name as well. I agree with your observation. There is so much more going on. I cannot go into details at this moment."

"What can you tell me? Will I be assigned? I will not leave Kemia. I don't care what happens….."

"Agreed. But I must tell you something before we continue. Are you listening?"

"I am listening."

"We have what humans call a sieve in our mist."

"It's a *leak*. How exciting. Angel spies." Both angels turned toward Kemia. "Oh, c'mon," she added, "I can only wash my hands and count the tiles so many times—928, by the way, and 54 are cracked—before boredom sets in. Besides," she said, grinning wickedly, "I gave you plenty of time to talk about me."

Rafayal could not help but laugh. Kemia radiated warmth and joy. Avial had been correct. This woman was very different from any human they had encountered. With a formal bow over her hand, Rafayal said, "My Lady Kemia Reid, it is an honor to meet you. Word has traveled of your deeds. My name is Rafe, at your service."

Xathaniel cocked his eyebrow at Rafayal and mouthed, *Rafe?*

"It's a pleasure to meet another angel. Have you and Nate been friends long?" Kemia asked.

Xathaniel chuckled and said quietly, "Cool nickname."

"Not even," Kemia replied. "Besides, we're not alone."

"Good point."

"Actually, *Nate* and I know each through a mutual friend. We are not officially friends, however, we have tremendous respect for each other." It was the only indication Rafayal gave that he had heard Xathaniel and Kemia's whispered exchange.

"So, you two don't talk or hang out, even though you have the same friend?" Kemia asked.

"Lady, not everyone has the same logic you do." Xathaniel took her hand and led her back to bed. He tucked the blankets around her form and then sat on the bed next to her. Rafayal took note of how natural Xathaniel cared for her and how she followed his lead.

"Forgive me for my forwardness. I know you both have lived so much longer than I, but it seems to me that if you have so many things plotting against you, you would need as many allies as possible. Not to mention, it could be a lonely existence. I have practically no friends, except now you guys, and it's pretty lonely. Sorry, I just had to say something. Hey, speaking of that, what's your mutual friend's name?"

"DJ," Rafayal answered before Xathaniel could speak. "His name is DJ. Why? Would you like to meet him?"

"Uh, no," Kemia said in surprise. "I just want to put a name to him and not refer to him as a third party. It's kind of rude and unkind."

"Lady Kemia, forgive me. We are running low on time. I was summoned to duty to your side."

"My side, why?"

"I am to give you the blessing of healing so that you and Xathaniel may leave this place." Rafayal turned to address Xathaniel. "Dark angels know of her; they seek to capture her. If they cannot, they will cease her life force."

"Do you mean kill me? Why?! I'm a nobody. I'm not important to anyone here!"

"Lady Kemia, you are the only human that can fight demons. It is a power that has never been blessed in a human. Now, I must give you a blessing of healing."

Rafayal walked to the side of the bed. He looked at Xathaniel. "Stand guard."

"Am I late?" Avial had suddenly appeared. "What is for breakfast? Did I say that right?" He laughed.

Rafayal turned to face the latecomer. "Uh, sir! It is an honor and privilege. I did not know you would be here."

If Kemia was aware of the tension between the angels, she gave no indication.

"Hey, Avial. Welcome back. Rafe was about to give me a blessing of healing. Isn't that sweet of him? If I wasn't stuck here … ya da, ya da."

Avial looked first at Xathaniel and then at Rafayal questioningly. "Is there anything I can do?" he asked.

"Stand watch with Xathaniel," Rafayal said.

Xathaniel and Avial took out their weapons. Xathaniel stood guard by the door, and Avial stood by the window. Kemia was happy. Not only did she have visitors, they were all handsome men. Kemia took a long look at Rafayal while he gave last-minute instructions to Xathaniel and Avial. He was yummy to look at: six foot three with long brown hair and piercing, green eyes. To Kemia, Rafe looked like the men she had seen at the gym—all hard planes and stocky. She looked at Xathaniel's dark hair and blue eyes—he was the only one who warmed her heart.

"Ready, Lady Kemia?"

"Yes. Thank you."

"For the blessing? It is no trouble. It is my duty."

"That too. Being my friend is not."

Rafayal looked deeply into Kemia's eyes. Behind her smile he found pain. He recognized it for what it was. Rafayal whispered, "How do you know I'm your friend?"

Kemia placed a hand on his cheek. "Because you laughed."

Rafayal smiled. "Lady Kemia, you are a true friend. Remember my instructions, warriors," he reminded, "and I'll begin."

"Yes, sir," Avial and Xathaniel said at the same time.

Rafayal placed both hands on top of her head and closed his eyes. Kemia followed his lead and closed her eyes as well. Just before he was about to begin, she cranked one eye open and looked up at him. "If this hurts, I will not share my dessert with you today." She closed her eyes again and then added, "Aw heck, yeah, I will. I'd hate to see a grown angel … not smile." Rafayal looked up to find the other two angels smiling widely.

"Duly noted," he said and reclosed his eyes. "Father, thank you for blessing me with another to call my friend. Please grant me the wisdom to follow your plan for all. Bless Kemia Reid with the same wisdom as her gifts develop." As Rafayal said the words out loud, but softly, his gift of healing was purging Kemia of her illness. Xathaniel and Avial could see her life force getting stronger. Rafayal continued his prayer. "Thank you for blessing my new friend with the talent of making others feel good about themselves. Amen."

"That was beautiful, Rafe. Amazingly so. I feel so much better."

Just then, a puff of black smoke appeared, and in its place was a blond man with gray eyes. Kemia disliked him instantly. He had an oily feel about him. She couldn't describe it; it just felt like he didn't belong around them.

"Then it's true, a monkey has the power of a child of fire," the man said.

Kemia leaped out of bed and stood in front of Rafayal protectively.

"Aw, poor baby. You don't think much of yourself, do you?" Kemia said softly. "Of course, if monkey is your name, I wish I could say, 'Nice to meet you, Monkey." Kemia spoke rather sweetly, but Xathaniel was not fooled by her demeanor.

"I've heard of you," the stranger said. "You're either very brave or very foolish."

While they were having their exchange, Xathaniel moved slowly to stand slightly in front of Kemia's right side, double angelic swords drawn.

"Avial. Xathaniel. My old brothers-in-arms."

"Azazel, Zophael would be disappointed in you, would he not?" Avial said sadly.

"Cousin, I'm more than disappointed in you. You are bowing down and serving creatures that can do nothing more than tricks. They are monkeys, and you serve them! What does that make you, Cousin?"

"You know the answer. A warrior of service. You just refuse to accept it—your problem, not mine."

Azazel gave Avial an evil, oily smile. "Yes," he said, "I've heard your pitiful excuses. How rude of me. Have you met my friends?" Black, shadowy figures made their way across the walls and floors. They solidified into humanlike forms.

Kemia's indrawn breath captured Xathaniel's attention. She didn't do it very loud. It was barely above a whisper. Without a word, he leaned back slightly.

"Nate," she whispered, "those are the yucky things from when I was a child."

"Are you certain, Fire?"

"Yes, no doubt."

Rafayal stood still and watched the whole exchange silently. He started to unsheathe his weapon to engage in battle. A gentle, loving voice in his head said, *Be easy, warrior; do not show your hand. All will be revealed in time. Still, warrior, still.*

Rafayal dropped his hands to his sides, drawing Azazel's attention. "Who is your friend without weapons? Could he be a nonservice? Come, Brother, let me show you the way."

"Like you showed Callie?!" Anger radiated from Avial.

"Ah, Cousin, you can still be with your sister. It's not too late."

"I have lost my sister to battle."

"So be it." Azazel spun around toward the demons. "Kill the warriors, and capture the monkey and the nonserver—he may be useful."

Kemia thought about how Avial had come and helped her when Xathaniel was in trouble. She thought about how Xathaniel had kept her company all night so that she didn't think about being sick and alone. And her thoughts turned to Rafe, the angel who gave her the beautiful blessing—she thought of his friendship and laughter. These three men had given her more than anyone had in her life.

No! This couldn't happen. They could not be allowed to take her new family. She had just found them. Kemia look directly at Azazel. "Leave them alone! You can't take my family!"

Xathaniel and Avial grinned. They had already felt a taste of Kemia's power. Rafayal looked stunned.

"Shut up, monkey. The higher beings are talking." Azazel grinned evilly.

"Name-calling. How trite. And I said *no!*" When Kemia said her last word, power unlike any of them had felt before came off her in waves. The creatures exploded and disappeared, and all the angels, including Azazel, fell to the floor, paralyzed. Xathaniel crawled over to Kemia and took her hand. Almost immediately, Rafayal and Avial were released.

Rafayal rose and stood in front of her. "Lady Kemia," he said, "I thank you. I am in your debt."

Kemia didn't respond. Her eyes remained on the dark angel on the floor. "Lady, we must go," Avial said. "There will be others. And we cannot block this room from human presence for much longer." Avial's voice was urgent. "You have weakened us."

Kemia still hadn't moved. Rafayal took in everything that had happened and finally pieced together what Kemia was doing. "As long as Xathaniel has physical contact with Kemia, we are safe. She is holding Azazel prisoner. Xathaniel, let her know we are safe."

"She can hear you," Xathaniel said, smiling.

"I can. I'm draining his power by half so that we can get a head start," Kemia said. All eyes were on her as she performed that task.

"How do you know how to do that?" Rafayal inquired. "Only an arc can perform that undertaking, and not many know that information." Kemia finished her task. Azazel lay on the floor, very still.

"To be honest, I don't know. After you gave me that blessing, things just started lighting up in my mind. I just know what to do. Instinct, you know?"

"I see," Rafayal said and turned to the two warriors who were flanking her like they were her personal guards. "You must first get her to the earthly garden. The ruling will be made there, and you will receive your instructions on what to do next. Be wary; they will do everything possible to capture her. If they cannot capture her, they will not hesitate in taking her life force on the spot." Rafayal turned to address Avial. "Do you have your team?"

"Yes, sir. I arranged it last evening. Forgive me if I do not tell you where we are going to meet. The less you know …"

Xathaniel nodded. "Agreed. Speaking of knowledge," he said, facing Kemia, "we are a family?" Kemia gave a sheepish, almost shy smile, but she did not respond.

Rafayal winked. "Do not worry, little sister. I like having a family. I never had one before." He touched her cheek gently. "I'm delighted in being blessed with one."

Kemia impulsively threw her arms around Rafayal. "Stop being so kind, and help me pack." She wiped the tears away. "All of you—help me pack so that we can get out of here. Rafe, grab that backpack. Avial, get that tiny bag, and load all the things from the shelf in the bathroom, and Nate, watch our friend there. Go!" Everyone scattered to do Kemia's bidding.

"Fire?"

"Yeah? What's up?"

"How far of a head start will we get from him?"

"No less than three days. Why? What's going on in that head of yours?

"Just trying to figuring out our journey."

As she was talking to Xathaniel, Kemia was packing her room. Both were unaware of Rafayal watching them closely. Avial returned to the room and handed her a small makeup bag, which she shoved in the side pocket of her backpack. Kemia went over to the wall locker, took out her purse, and removed her wallet, keys, cell phone, and checks. She placed the items in the rear pocket of the backpack and zipped it up. Next, Kemia wrote a quick note, tucked it in the purse, and left the purse on the bed. She glanced around one last time to make sure she hadn't forgotten anything.

Kemia smiled at the trio of angels. "I'm ready when you are," she said.

PART 2

*No one can make you feel inferior
without your consent.*
—*Eleanor Roosevelt*

CHAPTER 9

She couldn't believe it. She just couldn't believe it! But then again, reality had taken a dive twenty-four hours earlier. Had it really been only twenty-four hours? She felt it had been a lifetime. She shook her head. She was hanging out with angels. How *Twilight Zone* was that?

Kemia made it out of the hospital without any trouble, largely thanks to her protectors. As soon as she finished packing, the three of them had surrounded her and led her out of the building. What she couldn't believe was that no one bothered them or stopped them. Amazing!

They were in the parking lot at the far end of the hospital when Rafayal stopped walking. "I have to go, little sister. The young warriors will care for you."

"Rafe, will I see you again?"

Rafayal placed his hands on either side of her face and kissed her on her forehead. It was comforting. It brought to her mind a sense of someone looking out for her, taking care of her, making her feel less alone in the world.

"Rest easy. You will," Rafayal replied. "We are a family. Safe journey, and peace be with you, Kim." Rafayal had given her a nickname too. "Peace be with you, warriors," he continued. "Look after our adopted sister."

"Peace be with you, Rafe," Xathaniel said, returning the good-bye. Avial's head bobbed his farewell.

"As with you, big brother," Kemia sniffled. In a flash of light, Rafayal was gone.

She felt Xathaniel's hands on her shoulders. "Come. We must go."

Kemia took a few steps and snapped her fingers as if remembering something. "We need a vehicle. You know, something to travel in. I know you need to spread your wings every once in a while, and you can't do that in a crowd of people. And I can't fly, so we must travel by car and check in hotels along the way."

"Avial, what is a hotel?"

"I'll explain later, but first we must meet our team."

"And eat breakfast," chimed Kemia. "I'm starving. Remember—I'm the human here."

"So, Avial, what are we doing? You are the team leader."

"No, you are, sir."

"I was sent as guardian—nothing more. You put together the team; now you are the team leader."

Avial was staring at his longtime commander in awe. He never dreamed he would be in command one day. He always was happy to be by Xathaniel's side; it never occurred to him that he would have to leave it. "Well, being that we have to meet up with the rest of group immediately, that is where we will go."

"Can we zap there like you angels do?" Kemia asked. She was getting more excited with her adventure by the minute. It was obvious that she wanted to experience everything the angels did.

Xathaniel spoke first. "I am not willing to take that chance just yet. Wait until we can test you a bit without dark angels on our trail."

"Aw. Well, okay, if you think it's best."

"I do. Avial, are we ready?"

"Yes. How are we going to get there? The meeting point is 11.8 miles. We can do it with no effort, but Kim will have troubles."

"Guys, I can call a taxi. It will be your first ride in a car."

Kemia and Xathaniel turned to Avial expectantly. "All right, let's do it," he said.

Kemia made the call from her cell phone. She requested a van. She informed the dispatcher that they would be making two stops to pick up other passengers. Kemia was told it would take about ten minutes for the taxi to arrive. Meanwhile, she spotted an ATM and indicated that she wanted to get some money for travel. The men escorted her to the bank machine.

Once the taxi arrived, Kemia stepped aside and allowed Xathaniel to enter first. Ever the gentleman, he insisted that she go first—that is, until she explained that she wanted him to have the window seat. He grudgingly conceded. Kemia sat in the middle, and Avial took up the left side. Once settled, Kemia gave the driver the address to her apartment building.

She sat back to observe her companions. She looked to Avial first. He was calm and cool on the outside, but she was certain he was full of questions on the inside. Kemia knew he was making mental notes to question her at a later date. Sometimes understanding seemed to come too quickly, and she saw sadness blanket his eyes.

Kemia turned her attention toward Xathaniel. His eyes were darting around, taking everything in. He had a look of controlled excitement. That's when Kemia noticed it—they were not as excited from being in a vehicle as they were from simply observing their surroundings. Finally, the taxi pulled in front of the apartment building. She gave the driver his fare.

"Could you please wait for us? We have one more stop. If you can't, call for another van, please."

The driver nodded but did not speak. Kemia thanked him, gave him another twenty dollars, and exited the taxi. As she shut the door, she turned to find that the doorman to her building had stepped up to greet her.

"Martin," Kemia said, "how are your children and your wife? I understand you just added a little girl to your houseful of boys."

"Hello, Ms. Reid. Everyone's great. Yeah, her big brothers spoil her every chance they get." Martin walked over and opened the door to the lobby. They all filed in. "How are you, ma'am? You look better. Your parents were here last week to check on your place."

"Were they? I must thank them," she said sardonically. "Oh, Martin, I'm going on a little trip. I'm going to see a specialist abroad. Mr. Stanton will be here in a day or two. Brian Stanton. He will show you his identification. No one else, including my parents, is to be let into my apartment without written permission from Mr. Brian Stanton. You got the name?"

"Mr. Brian Stanton. Got it. I'll pass it onto the other doormen."

"That's fine. However, Brian will only come during your shift. If you are here with others, he will ask for you by name. And there is one more thing—and this part I ask you to keep to yourself, as a favor to me."

"Of course, Ms. Reid. You're the only tenant that asks about my family, and you always treat me real nice. The rest treat me like I'm one of the fixtures here. What can I do for you?"

Kemia looked at Martin seriously. "When Mr. Stanton arrives, give him this message: 'Even geniuses have their masters.' Please repeat that for me."

"Every genius have their master."

"No. Try again. 'Even geniuses have their masters.' Go."

"'Even geniuses have their masters.' Ms. Reid, are you in some kind of trouble?"

Kemia gave a little chuckle. "Not really. Mr. Stanton is my attorney, and I need to go on one last adventure. My parents have selfish reasons for me not to go, and if they find out I left for this treatment, they would strip me of my rights and lock me in a hospital until my illness robs me of my life." Kemia gave Martin a meaningful look. "You know what I mean?"

A look of horror came over his face. Kemia continued, "The money isn't as important as my freedom. It's why I'm trusting only you. You see, I know your secret, what happened to you and your wife in your own country. And I know what you had to do to free yourself. That is none of my business. I will make a promise to you, here and now: *no one* will harm you or your family again. I saw to that."

Martin stood stock-still. "Why?"

"You think I don't know about all the times you have looked after me. For example, the con artist who tried to date me for my money. There was nothing in it for you, yet you took care of business." Kemia felt Xathaniel's light touch. She glanced back at him and nodded. "I have to go. Would you please follow my instructions to the letter?"

"Yes, Ms. Reid." Kemia, Xathaniel, and Avial made their way across the lobby to the elevators. Before reaching their destination, Kemia stopped and turned. Martin rushed over. "Was there anything else, Ms. Reid?"

"Yes. The day I went into the hospital, it was your time off, so I didn't get a chance to give you this." In her hand was an envelope with a card inside. "My congratulations to you and your family." Martin open the envelope to find a five-hundred-dollar gift card to a local department store and a two-thousand-dollar check addressed to him. He was struck speechless. "I'm sure that will start a college fund for your kids. Good luck."

Martin smiled. "Yes, ma'am."

With that settled, Kemia rode the elevator to her apartment. It wasn't until she was inside that she let loose on the two angels.

"You could have warned me that you were 'going Casper'! I was arguing with you, and I didn't know you were invisible until we were halfway to our destination. The taxi driver was looking at me like I was nuts. I think the only thing that saved me was the money!"

Kemia was greeted with silence after her rant. She looked from Xathaniel to Avial and back. "What aren't you boys telling me?" she asked.

"You tell her; you are her favorite."

Xathaniel shook his head. "You are the leader."

"I do not want to know what a statue feels like," Avial whined.

"Oh, I see. You want the lead, not the consequences."

"Now, that is not fair. There were many times when you—"

"All right! Quiet!" Kemia's gaze bounced between the two. "How about you both tell me?"

"We are not allowed to be visible to others until the whole team is united." Avial rushed his words out.

"Okay, what's so bad? How many are on the team?"

"Counting me and Xathaniel? Five."

"Where are the other three?"

"On the roof. Kim, there is something you should know. Two of them are twin siblings."

Kemia raised her eyebrow in a silent *So what?*

"You see," he continued, "they have never been to Earth, and both have … tempers. One can control thunder, and the other has the duty of lightning. Asival—she has the duty of lightning; her twin brother, Pyriel, has been blessed with the duty of thunder. Our final team member is Peter. He is in training to become Xathaniel's assistant."

Xathaniel groaned. Avial continued with a wicked smile. "Yes, my friend, you are on your way to becoming an arc. Peter has the blessing of intuition and all the powers of a watcher. In other words, Lady, you have yourself a few children for a week or so."

"Is that all?" Kemia said. "No problem. Let's pack."

Xathaniel roared with laughter. "Famous last words."

CHAPTER 10

After one hour, Kemia was ready. She did a mental list: Change of clothes? Check. Cash, ATM debit card, and traveler's checks? Check. Passport? Check. Note of instructions for her lawyer? Double check.

She opened her Bible and put the instructions in the proper place. That's when Kemia noticed that it was entirely too quiet in her apartment. When she first went into her bedroom, she heard things being moved about in the other room and heard her windup music boxes being played. After fifteen minutes, she had heard the television set click on. The bluesy sound of the opening credits of Barney Miller had filled the air. Kemia relaxed. They were watching something safe. She chuckled to herself. *What do you know? Xathaniel was right. I do have children to watch.* Which brought her to her next thought. *It was way too quiet for two very curious angels.*

"What are you two doing in there?" she yelled from her bedroom.

Their response came in unison. "Nothing."

A sure sign that they were up to something. She picked up her oversized backpack and exited the bedroom. Upon arriving in the living room, she was greeted by the entire contains of her refrigerator spread out on the coffee table, including the condiments. Both men were sitting on the sofa, playing video games.

"*Ha!*" Xathaniel crowed. "You lost. You now have to eat three bites of the mystery dish."

Avial reached for the goose-liver pate. Just when he was about to take his first bite, Xathaniel advised, "Add the sweet relish; it will taste better." Avial nodded and did as he was instructed. He put the concoction in his mouth. Avial's eyes crossed, and his face looked like he had sucked on a sour lemon. Kemia couldn't help but laugh out loud.

Both men started in surprise at her laughter. They looked up and saw her leaning against the wall observing them.

Xathaniel grinned. "How long have you been there?"

Kemia grinned back. "Long enough to know men are children."

Avial look sheepish. "Hello, Kim. We were just playing your game."

"Looks to me like you were doing a little more than that, big brother."

Avial gave another sheepish smile but remained silent. Xathaniel noticed Kemia's bag at her feet. "I see you are ready to go."

"I am ready when you are. But first, let's clean up this mess. I don't want Pam to think I had a wild party."

"Who is Pam?" Avial inquired.

"She's my housekeeper. She makes everything clean, shiny, and new around here. I have her come in once a week." Kemia grabbed the kitchen wastebasket. She started dumping the open food-storage containers. Then she grabbed the fresh fruit and vegetables and returned them to their rightful place in her refrigerator. She handed the cartons of milk and juice to Xathaniel.

"Put them back," she said. Wordlessly, he did as requested.

Kemia turned to Avial and handed him the garbage bag. "Take this to the end of the hall, and put it in the trash compactor. It's marked Trash." Avial walked out the front door. While he was gone, Kemia wiped the glass coffee table with surface cleaner. When she was done, she put away the cleaning supplies and returned to the living room.

Both angels were waiting for her by the front door. She went to reach for her backpack, but Xathaniel beat her to it. They all exited the apartment. Kemia locked the door and engaged the alarm system. She turned and headed toward the elevator. That's when she noticed she was the majority of one. Kemia looked around and found them down the hall in front of a door marked Stairs. She raised her eyebrow inquiringly.

Xathaniel laughed. "Roof, remember? They are waiting for us. We'll take the stairs." He held out his hand, and Kemia captured it as they both started up the stairs. Kemia suddenly stopped.

"What is wrong?" Xathaniel asked.

"The taxi. I forgot the taxi."

Both looked at Avial for direction.

He sighed. "You cannot call down to cancel. We would be traced by shadow helpers."

"Wait. What are shadow helpers?"

Xathaniel grabbed Kemia's hand again and gave a little tug. "I will explain later. Right now, we must not keep the others waiting."

Avial watched them as they climbed the stairs ahead of him. What he was witnessing was truly amazing. He was watching his longtime friend fall in love. An angel's natural blessing is to love. But, as Avial watched, he realized that his friend, nay, his brother, was laughing more. He took note of Kemia. She was chatting animatedly to Xathaniel, and Xathaniel was listening to her with an amused smile on his face. He held their clasped hand, her left in his right, over his heart.

Suddenly, a wave of sadness came over Avial. *Angels are not allowed to be with the sons of Adam and daughters of Eve. If they do, they will fall*, he thought miserably. Maybe it was selfish of him, but he did not want to lose his friend. A powerful, yet gentle voice in his head said, *Do not despair, my warrior. All will be revealed in due time.* Avial smiled to himself and looked up to find Kemia on the landing above, staring at him worriedly. He gave her a warm smile. If he was to choose a helpmate for his brother, he could do no better than this woman.

"Are you okay?" she asked.

"I am good; thank you," Avial said.

"I sent Xathaniel ahead." Avial glanced up above Kemia's head and barely contained his laughter. Xathaniel was not too far from the landing. Of course, he would be protective of his new family. Avial knew for a fact that Xathaniel had no other family to speak of.

Kemia continued, "I felt your sadness. What's wrong, big brother?" She repeatedly surprised him with her extraordinary blessings.

He gave her a brilliant smile. "I am well, little sister. I merely got lost in my thoughts."

"Is there anything I can help with?"

Avial looked into Xathaniel's eyes and then looked back at her. "Just continue to make my only brother as happy as he seems to be today." Kemia turned to find Xathaniel four steps above her. The men were sharing something that she was not privy to. This did not bother her; these two had been friends for a long time, maybe longer than she could ever dream of.

She smiled. "I shall do my best. Now, I have a question."

Avial chuckled. "Here we go. Go on—ask."

Kemia rolled her eyes and ignored his teasing. "Do you want more brothers?" She turned around and continued up the stairs to the roof. Avial looked at her back, puzzled. He ran to catch up with her. Once again, he noticed the couple's clasped hands, this time, her right in his left, as he reached her left side.

"What do you mean?" Avial inquired.

"I mean would you be happy with more friends you regard as brothers—as you do Xathaniel?"

Both men froze on the stairs to stare at her. "Did I say something wrong?" Kemia glanced from one man to the other. "Xathaniel?" Her eyes rested on Xathaniel.

Xathaniel took their clasped hands up to his lips and kissed the back of her hand. "No, Lady, you did nothing wrong. You just surprised us yet again."

"I don't get it. How?"

"Can I do the honors of explaining this, Xathaniel?" Xathaniel dipped his head to concede. "You see," Avial continued, "humans are under the impression that all angels are friends and know each other. But when the civil war began, loyalties were questioned. Brothers were no longer brothers. Childhood friends could not be friends. So the warrior's life became a lonely existence."

"I got that from Rafe when he blessed me." She turned and continued up the stairs steadily. Kemia left in her wake two very surprised and confused angels.

They caught up to her. "Kim, would you be kind enough as to explain that," Avial asked. He was curious.

Kemia smiled. "Oh, that. Well, when Rafe gave me a blessing, it was like a dam broke in my head. I felt stronger, and the history of your wars seemed to light up my head." She suddenly turned toward Xathaniel for answers. "Why is that, Nate?"

Xathaniel took her face in his hands, and he gazed into her eyes. "I do not know, my Lady, but I make this promise: I will find out."

She gave a dazzling smile. "If you say so. So, how did you and Avial become friends?"

Avial gave a sad smile. "That is a sad story. You see, I have always looked up to my cousin, you know, the one we encountered, but he began to get angry when I was assigned to the watchers. Once I started my tenure with the watchers, I did not have as much time with my sister as I would have liked. Most of my time was spent on my assignments. Azazel"—he choked on the name—"Azazel started talking to my sister, Calinda. She was a half sister but my sister no less. She was a child of earth, not one of fire. He did not know this, and he filled her mind full of power. Do you remember what I told you about the children of Adam and Eve?"

"Yes. They can be greatly influenced, right?"

"Correct. And because we all have freedom of choice, Azazel's influence over Calinda was great. She chose to stay with him because she knew nothing of service and the many blessings that come with it."

"Two questions."

Avial nodded his consent.

"First question. What will happen when Azazel and the others find out that she's what they despise? Second question. What do you mean by blessings that come with service? I know the saying that everything you do comes back to you tenfold."

"We do not know what will happen to Calinda," Xathaniel cut in. "So we are waiting. You would think after 592 years, Azazel would have figured it out."

Kemia said thoughtfully, "You know, he may know, but he may choose not to acknowledge the info."

Avial looked at her with a puzzled frown. "What do you mean? I cannot imagine Azazel being forgiving when it comes to humans."

"Me either. Follow me for a minute or two. He knows what your sister meant to you, and probably still means to you, so maybe he's too busy having a good time taunting you. Is your sister the only family you have?"

"No. You know of my brother, Arvial. My parents decided to take the fall."

"Yes, I could never forget Arvial. See, I rest my case. As long as you react to him throwing in your face the fact your sister chose him over you, he's going to keep doing it—especially if it bothers you."

As the trio made their way up the last of the stairs and out the trapdoor, Kemia paused and turned toward Avial. "Please forgive me ahead of time if I offend. I have something I need to say to you."

In the two days that he had known Kemia, he could already tell that she was not a being that would hurt others. Has it really only been two days? Avial felt he had been her big brother for a millennium. When had he stopped thinking of her as a child of earth? Avial gave her a genuine warm smile. "You could never offend me, little sister. Say what is in your heart."

"Well, okay. It seems to me that ever since your cousin hijacked your family, he has had control over you." At Avial's puzzled expression, Kemia continued. "It is said that our past can dictate our future, right?"

"I get that much."

"Well, the past cannot be changed but our future can. Forgive, but don't forget—because there are always lessons to be learned—and move on."

Avial never dreamed of looking at his situation so simply before. Maybe he was making things more complicated than they needed to be. Avial reached out and hugged Kemia. "Did I ever tell you that you are the best sister in the world?"

"Should I take offense to that?"

The duo turned and faced a young woman with blue-black, curly, shoulder-length hair; green eyes that sparkled with coldness; and a figure to make a supermodel cry with envy.

"Hello, big brother. I heard you missed me," she said.

"You are no sister of mine," Avial replied.

"So this fat monkey is?! I heard you! You called her your sister!"

All the things that Kemia had talked to him about resurfaced. Avial smiled when he realized that what she had said was true—they took pleasure in taunting him.

Calinda was getting angry. Why wasn't he acting like he usually did? It was the girl! The female monkey! Calinda had heard about her, so she thought she would see what the fuss was about. Calinda appraised the girl. What she saw was a woman with a size 18 body, light-brown eyes, and auburn hair. She refused to acknowledge that Kemia was very pretty. She glared at her with hatred.

"You will step away from my brother, monkey!"

Kemia looked angrily at Calinda. "*No name-calling!*" Her shout brought the other four angels from where they had been meeting. Everyone felt the power build around Kemia.

"Quick! Hold hands!" Xathaniel shouted. Without hesitation, all the angels held hands, forming a loose line. Xathaniel grabbed Avial's hand into one of his, and with the other, he touched Kemia's lower back. The power built up around them. Suddenly, it slammed into Calinda. She fell wordlessly to the ground, still.

"My Fire! It's me! Draw it in, my heart!" Xathaniel was speaking into Kemia's ear. The level of her powers went lower and lower, until Xathaniel no longer felt he was being weighed down.

He turned to Avial. "What happened?"

"We came behind you from the stairs, so engrossed in our chat that we did not see Calinda until it was too late. She, of course, taunted me, and Kim got angry. You know the rest."

Xathaniel took Kemia in his arms and hugged her tight. "It is over."

"She'll be out for four days."

"Why so long?"

"She is the greatest threat to our mission."

Xathaniel nodded. "Kim, meet the rest of the team. First, may I present Asival?"

"I thought my temper was something! I heard of you, Sister." She shook Kemia's hand.

"As have I, little sister," said her twin. "You are quickly becoming a legend. Pyriel, at your service."

"All right, how is it that so many people have heard about me in such a short time? And I want to know what is being said."

"Only that you are different from anything we have encountered. You are kindhearted, beautiful, and blessed with powers to hunt demons." Kemia turned toward the voice. She was looking into the dark-blue eyes and curly, golden-blond hair of a young man who looked like he should hardly be out of high school. Kemia tipped her head to the side.

"You must be Peter," she said.

"I am, Lady."

"Call me Kim. I'm starting to like that name."

"Kim, we best get out of here," Pyriel said, looking around uneasily. "There could be more, and we want to be far ahead of them."

"Okay, first we need a vehicle, and then we need food and a couple of hotel rooms for the night. I have cash and traveler's checks, so we will not be traced for at least twelve to twenty-four hours."

Avial thought for a moment. "Let us flash to rent a car, and then Kemia will drive us to food. We'll work out the details during our trip. Is that an agreeable plan, Guardian?"

Xathaniel, deep in thought, sighed. "We have no choice. I would like to test and practice Kim's blessings before we use our angelic blessings with her. It looks like we will have to do things quickly."

Xathaniel took Kemia's hand and kissed it before they disappeared in a shower of silver light.

"Brother, did you see the way Xathaniel looked at her? I have never seen that before," Asival said.

Pyriel smiled, for there was a woman that he looked at in the very same way—Kemia had her same smile.

"Yes, Sister, I did," he said.

And the rest of the angels disappeared in a flash of silver light.

CHAPTER 11

Kemia rented a full-sized van without any problems. "Now I'm going to take you to my favorite steakhouse."

"What is a steakhouse?" a voice behind her inquired.

Since she was driving and Xathaniel was sitting in the passenger seat, she couldn't determine whether the voice belonged to Peter or Pyriel, so she answered to no one in particular. "It's an eating place."

Xathaniel's eyes lit up. "You all will like food. Most of it is very tasty."

Kemia pulled up into the parking lot and parked the van in one of the slots. "Okay, everybody out. Follow me."

"Into hell, if you wish, my Fire."

"Stop flirting, and get out." Kemia giggled.

The angels in the backseat shared grins. Kemia and Xathaniel got out and reached for each other's hands automatically. The couple was oblivious to the meaningful looks being exchanged among the other angels.

When they entered the restaurant, the host greeted them. "Welcome. I hope you are having a great day. How many are in your party?"

"Six, please, and thank you. May we have a big table? I have a feeling my companions will be ordering a lot of food." Kemia smiled.

"Of course!"

The group followed the host to a round table big enough to seat ten people. "Will this be all right?" he asked.

"Perfect."

"Your servers will be here momentarily to take your order." With that, he went back to his duties at the front desk.

Kemia picked up the menu. "Mind if I order for us all? I know the menu inside and out. This is, after all, my favorite place."

They all looked at each other and then at Xathaniel. They trusted him. Xathaniel took Kemia's hand. "Please show us your place."

"All righty, I'm going to order everyone something different so that we all can try something of everything. Agreed?"

"Agreed," was said in unison.

Two servers turned up a moment later. Kemia smiled. "I have been elected to give everyone's order since I come here all the time."

Kemia pointed to Pyriel first. "He will have lemon-ginger lemonade, half ice, and the sirloin steak with seasoned fries. No salad, soup—he'll take the shrimp-and-lobster chowder."

Kemia placed her hand on Asival. "She'll have grilled chicken and a sweet potato with cinnamon, sugar, and butter; a grilled chicken and strawberry salad; and a nonalcoholic margarita to drink—blended— with lots of salt on the rim."

She smiled at Peter. "I know what you will like. Peter will have the Atlantic salmon with a fresh vegetable medley, a mixed green salad, and a root beer to drink."

Kemia placed her hand on Avial. "My big brother will have the top sirloin, green beans, and rice pilaf. To drink, he will have limeade."

Kemia turned and smiled at Xathaniel. "He will have an orange Sprite to drink, the porterhouse steak, mac 'n cheese, and green beans."

Xathaniel kissed Kemia on the back of her hand. "Thank you, Kim. We are all grateful that you are such a good friend."

Kemia laughed. "You are just saying that because I'm feeding you."

"Miss, what about you? Your order, please?"

"Silly me. I always forget about myself. I'll take the bone-in ribeye, grilled corn on the cob—make that two—and a strawberry Sprite to drink."

"How do you want your steaks cooked?"

"Medium rare all the way around," Kemia replied. The server left them to fill the order.

"Now that we have our food coming," Avial said urgently, "Peter, would you do the honor of placing a privacy bubble around us?" Everyone at the table felt the shift in power.

"Done."

"Good. Now to business. Now that we are all together, our mission is to take Kemia to the first garden. Safely, of course. I do not know why this is important, but it is."

"Wait. Why am I to go there? I don't get it. And what is this 'first garden' place?" Kemia looked to Xathaniel for answers.

"Lady, we are your protectors. We are in your service until we reach our destination. Do you remember what I told you about angels being in service?"

Kemia responded quietly. "Yes. Do what you must." Xathaniel placed a gentle hand under her chin and looked into her eyes.

"What is it? What is bothering you?"

"I don't feel right, letting you all put your lives in danger for me."

The table burst with laughter. "Little sister, you truly are a gem." Avial grinned. "We do this every day as battle warriors, and you have become an honorary warrior. I have not seen anyone take down Azazel since our younger years."

Kemia grinned. "He did make it easy by opening his mouth."

With a round of chuckles, the tension was released. Avial continued to fill everyone in on the mission. "Guardian, I know it will difficult, but you must make Kim the first priority—especially in battle. She is our mission. Without her, all is lost."

"I am called to service. It will be my honor to be in service," Xathaniel said solemnly. The script on his service gauntlets changed from brown, black, and bronze in color to silver and red.

Peter was the first to notice. "Um, excuse me, but I haven't been in warrior service as long as you all have been; what does that mean?" All eyes focused on what Peter was pointing to. Xathaniel touched his service gauntlets gently.

Peter looked over at Pyriel. "Red? You are the oldest of us all. Have you ever seen red in the service gauntlets?"

Pyriel looked from Kemia to Xathaniel and back again. There was amazement in his voice when he answered. "You are in blood service," he said to Xathaniel.

Kemia spoke before anyone else could. "Blood service? What's that? Is it as morbid as it sounds?"

Pyriel looked around the table. "Before I answer, let me explain. Blood service was gotten rid of over eighteen hundred years ago. Because of the nature of that service oath, we were losing more angels to death."

"Hold on, Brother," Asival interrupted. "For as long as I can remember, angels do not die; they just evolve into something new or different."

Pyriel look sad when he continued. "That is why blood service was discontinued. Angels died if the service was broken for any reason. Blood service is like a blood oath, only your life is given freely for the service."

In the time it took Pyriel to explain away his sister's objections, Kemia got very worried. "*No!* You can't do that!" The other angels felt her power began to build. "*Please* take it back. The oath. Take it back!"

"Ah, my darling Fire, I wouldn't want to. I made the oath with all the love and faith that I have to offer you." Xathaniel smiled as he brushed the tears from her face. Kemia threw her arms around his neck.

"I'm going to lose you after your service is up with me," she said.

"You misunderstand, little sister. Xathaniel will not die unless he deserts his duties as your guardian."

"Pyriel, I am confused. Tell us plainly what just happened," Avial demanded.

"All right. Xathaniel is in blood service to Kim. This is unusual two reasons: one, because no angel could ever go into blood service with a human, and two, because blood service oaths have not been honored in over eighteen hundred years. The silver shows it is sanctioned by a very high authority and the red is blood. The binding words that he spoke sealed it. As long as he honors his service, he will be fine."

A collected sigh of relief went around the table. "I am so glad my service gauntlets remain the same," Avial teased. He pulled his sleeve up to flash them to the group. Once again, quiet descended around the table. Avial's smile vanished as he noticed his gauntlets for the first time. The bronze and black were there as usual, but now there was silver too, with traces of teal. Everyone glanced over at Pyriel for answers.

"Sorry, family; this time I have no answers for you," he said.

"Things are really changing." Avial pulled his sleeve down to cover his gauntlets. "I do not think it is a bad thing; do you?"

He was greeted with silence. Kemia broke it. "No. I don't think so at all. Just different. Look—I met all of you. I went from not having practically anyone to having every one of you." She turned and looked Xathaniel in the eyes. "And I wouldn't change that for the world."

"Aw, that's so sweet!" Avial said as he started making gagging sounds.

"Keep it up and I will *not* order dessert for you," Kemia said sweetly.

Avial pretended to keel over and die. "Such cruelty. Good-bye, world."

Once again the table erupted into laughter. At that moment, their food began to arrive. The angels took great pleasure in the good food, drink, and company. They kept ordering more and more from the menu. Kemia had to put a stop to it after three hours. She paid the check with her debit card and left a generous tip for the servers.

By the time they exited the restaurant, it was dark. The group were making their way to the van when a shift in power erupted again.

"Hello, husband. I see you're treating our daughter well." A woman had appeared, and she turned her head toward Kemia. "Hello, child. I am your mother."

Kemia yelled, "*Nooooooooo!*" And then she laughed. "Is that what you wanted?"

The woman spun on Pyriel. "Did you teach her to disrespect her parent? Whether I'm a dark angel or not, she must learn some respect!"

Kemia's expression changed, and she faced Pyriel with hurt-filled eyes. "Is that true? Are you my father?"

Kemia and the rest of the traveling group looked at Pyriel expectantly.

"We have to talk," was Pyriel's tense response.

"We are talking!" The power built up in their small group. It was much stronger than Xathaniel had felt before.

"Kim," Xathaniel said softly. In one word he projected a wealth of emotion.

"I'm fine, Nate." Her eyes never left Pyriel. "Begin talking." The power surged up another notch.

"My, my, she does have your temper, husband."

Rumbling began in the skies above. Pyriel's eyes took on the blue-gray color of thunder clouds. Swirls of black danced dangerously in his eyes.

"*Do not call me your husband, demon! I am nothing to you but your enemy!*" Anger and power simmered around him. The rumble of thunder was getting louder.

Kemia looked at the pair with questions in her eyes.

A tinkle of laughter leaked out of the unknown dark angel's lips. To anyone else, it might have come across as cute and sexy; to Kemia, it was annoying.

"Ah, yes. Semantics, is it not?" The dark angel waved her hands in the air as if to swat away Pyriel's words like they were an annoying fly. "I'm her mother; you're her father. Therefore, *we* are her family. Come to Mother, my dear."

"*Enough!*" Asival shouted. Before anyone could react, she zapped the dark angel with a bolt of lightning. The woman collapsed wordlessly to the ground.

All eyes swung to face Asival. She grinned sheepishly. "Racheal always did annoy me," she said. She turned toward her brother. "I hope you do not mind, Brother. I had to take matters into my own hands. We have twelve hours before she wakes. She will seek us again." Asival glanced over at the silent Kemia and continued, "I suggest you have that talk with our little sister soon."

"You are correct, and I thank you, Sister," Pyriel responded quietly.

"Okay. Time to go," Kemia said to the group at large.

Pyriel looked at each member of the team to gauge his or her reaction to the recent events. As always, Asival looked like she would hurt anyone that would do harm to her brother. Avial was sneaking worried looks toward Kemia. Peter's gaze was bouncing back and forth between him and Kemia with sadness. It was clear that Peter wanted to say something to them both, but he resisted. Xathaniel had Kemia's hand pressed against his chest as they walked. He was talking to her in low voice about something privy to them. Kemia's face was impassive, but the power around her had not dissipated.

With a wave of his hand, the thunder moved on. His sister was correct; he must talk to Kemia Reid.

PART 3

"Our deepest fear is that we are inadequate
Our deepest fear is that we are powerful beyond measure
We were born to make manifest the glory of God that is within us"
—Marianne Williamson

CHAPTER 12

On the ride from the restaurant to the hotel, Kemia remained stubbornly silent. Xathaniel repeatedly tried to engage her in conversation. She did her best to hold back the tears that threatened to come out. While she was driving, she saw Xathaniel motion to the rest of the angels to remain silent. As far as she could tell, they all obeyed. She tuned out everyone so that she could concentrate on driving and not crying.

Upon arriving at the hotel, Kemia registered for three rooms, all doubles, for two nights. She asked the clerk to put the rooms side by side. The clerk complied. She paid cash. Xathaniel and Avial shared one room; she and Asival shared the middle room; and Peter and Pyriel went into the last. Kemia showed everyone how the showers and televisions work, and then, without a word to anyone, she left.

Kemia stood on top of the roof of the hotel—with angels nearby, no doubt. She stared at the stars. She tried not to think about what she had found out earlier—she wasn't an orphan; she had parents. Her mind would not allow her peace. All of the questions that she needed answers to were doing a mad, wild dance in her mind. If she was Pyriel's daughter, why had she been deserted? Was the dark angel really her mother? Why, after thirty-four years, did they think they could show up and be parents? Those questions pricked on her nerves. Kemia wanted answers, but she was unwilling to face them just yet. Suppose she was a product of a bad relationship? Tears made twin tracks down her face.

Two strong arms snaked their way around her waist and drew her back against a solid chest. Xathaniel didn't say a word. Kemia didn't either; she snuggled into his arms. He rocked her to and fro.

"Why?" Kemia asked, barely above a whisper.

"You would have to seek Pyriel for those answers."

Kemia buried her face in Xathaniel's shoulder and inhaled his scent. He smelled of fresh earth, cloves, and cinnamon. Oh how she loved those fragrances. She closed her eyes. The scent comforted her in ways she did not understand. Xathaniel stroked her hair gently before he spoke.

"My Fire, what would you like to do?"

Kemia started. No one had ever asked her what she wanted. When she was in the group home, her adopted parents had chosen her. Once that was settled, her schools and activities were picked for her, including what college she was to attend. Her job had fallen into her lap. Kemia later found out that her adoptive father had called in a favor. When she got sick, her adoptive parents took over almost everything that needed to be done, from the choice of hospital to the doctor she was to see. Kemia don't know why she had allowed it to go on. Check that—she knew why. She didn't want to rock the boat for fear they wouldn't want her. Understandably, she was proud of the two things that hadn't been picked out for her: her newfound friends and her lawyer.

And now she, Kemia Denise Reid, was being asked what *she* wanted. She drew a blank. Her brain short circuited with all the possibilities.

Xathaniel chuckled. Kemia felt his whole body shake when he did so.

"Okay. How about this: would you like to meet with Pyriel?"

"I don't know, Bear. There are things swirling round and round in my head. I'm so angry—and so scared. I'm scared that he will reject me or that I'll hurt him." Kemia looked down at the ground in shame. "I know he's good, and I want to preserve the things that I know are good. It sounds naïve, but it's me. I am naïve about so many things. I choose to be. But make no mistake, I do and will take care of business."

Xathaniel sighed and rubbed Kemia's arms in comfort. "Fire, I hate to state the obvious, but you will never get your answers until you ask Pyriel your questions."

Kemia rolled her eyes and blew out her breath. "Did anyone ever accuse you of beating a dead horse?"

Xathaniel chuckled. "Does that mean you have made up your mind?"

Kemia laughed. "Yes, Captain Obvious."

Xathaniel sobered. "It is good to hear you laugh. Your sadness and anger were so suppressing." Kemia felt tension that she didn't realize he was holding leave his body. "I was afraid that I would not see that three-million-watt smile again," he said. "For a few hours, it was down to three thousand."

Kemia burst out laughing. "Where in the world did you hear that expression?"

Xathaniel looked down at her warily. "Did I use it incorrectly? The television was talking about light bulbs and wattages. They said the higher the wattage, the brighter the light. Does that apply to smiles?"

She turned in his arms to face him. She placed her hand on his cheek and gazed into his eyes. "What you said is beautiful. I am not used to men talking to me like you do. In fact, no man has looked at me the way you do."

Xathaniel roared with laughter. "You are joking, right?" At her serious look, he stopped laughing instantly and stared at her in shock. "I thought that you were jesting," he croaked.

"Why would that be so hard to believe? Men would rather have women resembling Calinda or Asival, not me. They are both under size 10, and I'm the perfect size 18W. I'm the girl with the personality. You wanna know the best thing about my illness? I used to be size 26W. And felt no man saw anything other than a fat girl."

Xathaniel's face clouded over, and his eyes darkened with anger. The low hum of power radiated around him. Kemia jumped, a bit startled by his change of continence. She wasn't sure if he was angry at the mention of the dark angel or the other things that were being discussed. It was the first time Xathaniel had shown any kind of temperament.

"They are fools. And that is my great fortune. But this is not what angers me. What angers me is you. I will not allow anyone, including you, to put down my heart, my choice, my friend."

Kemia shook her head in denial. "Don't get me wrong. I like me. I'm my own best friend. I can live with what I've been and love what I am becoming. But I am not so arrogant as to expect it to be contagious."

The power surrounding Xathaniel dissipated as his brow furrowed. "I see," he said gravely.

She had expected him to say more. "Are you still upset with me?" He shook his head in the negative. Kemia threw herself at him, and he caught her in a bear hug. "Nate, why do you look so puzzled?"

"Just processing information. Kim, you do have a different outlook on things." Kemia wrapped her arms around his waist and burrowed deeper in his warmth. Xathaniel gave a little laugh.

"What's so funny, Bear?"

"Does this mean I need medical attention if I like you as you are?"

Kemia made a noise of impatience. "Of course not!"

"Good," Xathaniel whispered. "By the way, new nickname?"

Kemia giggled. "Just that one. And it's an old nickname."

He drew back slightly. "Kemia Reid, how long had you a private name for me?"

She couldn't contain her laughter. "Oh, don't be such a wet blanket," she said once she'd gotten her laughter under control. "I've had it all along. I just thought it would be more fun to tease you a bit."

"I'm listening. It is time for you to tell me all."

"When Rafe gave me the blessing, I couldn't help but think of you as *Honey Bear*. Honey, because you're so sweet and like food so much. Bear, because of your fierce, protective nature. Together, it's Honey Bear. But I'll only call you Bear. You'll know the rest, and it will make you smile. Do you like it?"

He tightened his hold and looked down at her with liquid blue eyes. "You have no idea how much." Xathaniel paused, as if to consider something. "Did I tell you why I do not want to be an arc—archangel as you humans call it?"

Xathaniel didn't talk about himself often, if at all. Kemia wanted to know every morsel about him. She was interested in the lives of all of her angel friends, but she wanted to know everything about Xathaniel. She knew in her heart that he could never be hers. Once he was done with his assignment, his Service Gauntlet returns to normal. He would officially be released from her service. Kemia would do her best to let him go. She knew he had duties in heaven, and she knew he was needed. Kemia would savor the memories for her hours alone. She would relive her adventures with her angels again and again; it would be like replaying her favorite movie.

"No. Tell me." She pulled him to sit next to her on what looked like a metal box.

"Well, it is rather difficult to talk about, but I will try. I do not want to sound vain. For some reason, I am highly … regarded," Xathaniel said with a crooked grin. Once again, she got the feeling he was not telling her everything. "Everywhere I go I hear whispers of hero worship, envy, and even fear. I detest it all. Can you imagine how much worse it will be when I assume being an arc? And I was just informed that I will also serve on the Council of Angels."

Kemia looked shocked. "That happens among angels! I would think they would be above all of those things."

"Why? We angels are in the middle of a civil war on top of the original war against evil. War is a very human reaction to disputes, is it not? Why can't angels feel anger, envy, and so forth?"

Kemia shrugged. "I never thought about it, to be honest. I'm afraid I suffer that human failing."

"As I was saying," Xathaniel continued, "I did my assignments as instructed and to the best of my abilities. I never paid any attention to the assignments or service. I just did them. Service makes me feel like I have a purpose. To me, I was doing my duty. I am good at what I have been blessed with, and it makes me uneasy when my fellow angels behave like I am different from them." Xathaniel turned toward Kemia to gauge her reaction and found her eyes filled with tears.

"What is wrong?" he asked with alarm.

"Nothing," she said, wiping her eyes. "I feel so ashamed for what I said earlier. You know, doubting how deep you feel for me. Bear, can you forgive me? I promise to prove my worth to you."

"Silly woman." Xathaniel pulled her out of her seat into a fierce hug. "Of course I do. You prove your worth every moment. Besides, I never took you seriously anyway." He placed a soft kiss across her lips. Kemia's body went iron straight and stiffened.

"You just kissed me."

"Nothing gets past you." Xathaniel laughed. "Yes, I did."

"It was our first kiss," Kemia whispered.

"Not yet. However, I can fix that." Xathaniel dipped his head and pressed his lips firmly on hers.

Kemia closed her eyes. She felt like she was floating. She put everything she was feeling for him into that kiss. She started to feel warm all over. When Xathaniel pulled away, Kemia had a hard time catching her breath.

You are so beautiful. I hope you love me as I love you. I just want to keep you safe, Kemia heard.

Wow! I felt that all the way to my feet! I wonder—do all angels kiss like that? I hope not. I want our kiss to be special. I want to remember this, us, when he has to go back to heaven, Xathaniel heard.

"What did you say?" they both said unison. They stared at each other.

"You can read my mind!" Kemia exclaimed.

Xathaniel grinned. "No, angels cannot typically read minds. They could in the past, but no more. It is only blessed when needed for service." He winked. "Just for the record, I do not know if angels kiss like we did. You were my first."

Kemia's heart melted. She didn't know how it happened, but she had fallen for this guy hard. Had it only been two days since they had met? How could you fall in love in two days? Then the impact of being able to read each other's mind sank in.

"Whoa!" Kemia jumped away from Xathaniel. She had asked the universe for one last adventure. It was a good lesson: be careful for what you wish for—you might get it in spades!

Xathaniel took one of Kemia's hands into both of his. "We must train tomorrow. Do not tell anyone of our new blessing. I would like to test it to see if it is temporary or permanent."

"Oooooo, does that mean more kissing? Sign me up for testing!"

He laughed and pulled her into his embrace.

I can get used to this, Kemia thought.

"So can I, my Fire; so can I," Xathaniel said out loud.

CHAPTER 13

Pyriel climbed onto the hotel roof. He spotted Kemia and Xathaniel on the other side with their heads together. He could not help but smile at them. They had fallen for each other hard. He knew that in over nine hundred years of service, Xathaniel had never even glanced at a woman, angel or otherwise. Although he and Xathaniel were not friends until recently, he was very much aware of the young angel's activities. How could he not be? Xathaniel was the talk among angels. He had become even more of a legend and mystery when no female angel could attract any attention other than politeness.

Pyriel gave a deep sigh. He could not put off his talk, although he was tempted to just play ignorant of all that had been revealed. With another sigh, he started to walk toward them, but then he stopped and turned around to head back to his room. He had left Peter watching the Discovery and the Disney channels in fascination. Pyriel stopped and reversed his steps to start toward the couple once again. They were so involved in their own world that they failed to notice him or his dilemma. A little less than halfway there, he froze again. *I need to talk to her. I need to make her understand*, he thought to himself.

"What am I doing?" Pyriel muttered.

"I will make a wild guess: wearing a hole through the roof?"

Pyriel started. He realized Avial was sitting on the air units.

"What are you doing here? Sneaking up on me?" Pyriel asked irritably.

Avial hopped down from the unit. "How could I sneak up on you when I was here first?"

"I have to agree," Asival said as she came from the shadows.

Avial laughed softly. "What are you doing here?'

"Just as you would not leave his side," Asival said, indicating Xathaniel, "I would not leave my brother's."

"All right, that means Peter is—" Before Avial could finish his statement, Peter materialized behind the trio.

"I am not staying down there by myself," Peter said in an almost childlike manner. "Besides, there are no more brownies."

"It is like a party," Pyriel said and grinned.

Avial laughed. "Who has the chips?" he said. Three angels looked at him blankly. "Sorry. Bad joke."

Pyriel turned to look at Kemia. She and Xathaniel were in an intense conversation, so they didn't hear the commotion that was going on across the roof.

"If you keep making excuses, you will never be able to talk to her. Just be honest, and she will welcome you," Avial said quietly. "My sister is warm and loving. She cannot stay angry at anyone for more than a day."

Pyriel turned to find three sets of eyes on him. Asival nodded. "Yes, she is more hurt than angry."

She motioned with her hands for her brother to go on.

He sighed deeply. *I can do this,* he thought to himself. He concentrated on putting one foot in front of the other. Without realizing it, Pyriel was repeating the phrase softly to himself as a mantra. After a dozen and one half steps—he had counted—Pyriel glanced up into the liquid eyes of Kemia. She looked as if she had been crying—a lot. Pyriel shuffled his feet and refused to meet her eyes.

"May we talk?" he asked. "I do not want to disturb you if you are busy."

"Sure. I have so many questions. Where do I begin?" Kemia had her back to Xathaniel's front. He had his arms securely around her waist. Once again, Pyriel had to admit that they really belonged together. She looked up at Xathaniel with her question. He simply smiled, brushed a soft kiss across her temple, and whispered something in her ear. She burst out laughing and playfully slapped his hands.

Pyriel thought he heard Kemia murmur, "Stop it, Bear. Behave." But he could have been mistaken. Pyriel cleared his throat. The couple turned to face him.

"Sorry. My first question is this: why did you leave me?"

A look of tremendous pain came across Pyriel's face. "I am so sorry! I had no choice. I was summoned to service. I left you with someone

I thought I could trust. I left you in a very safe place. I did the best I could with the short notice I had and with what I had available."

Kemia gave a bitter laugh. "Oh, yeah! The 'best I could' speech. The 'get out of trouble with your children' wild card." She pulled away from Xathaniel and began pacing in front of both angels. Power began to build around them all. She continued, "So let me get this straight—you left your daughter alone so that you could serve mankind? As your daughter, I needed you as much as anyone could!" Tears were streaming down her face.

Xathaniel took her hand. "Easy, Kim," he said. The power around them toned down a bit.

Wait! What did she say? Pyriel did a double take. "Lady Kemia, are you under the impression that I am your parent?"

Kemia nodded. "Um, yeah. Isn't that why you wanted to talk?"

"I would be honored to have you as my daughter—however, I am not your father. Racheal and I never been married. I thought it was explained to you that Dark Angels do not tell the truth unless it causes destruction"

"*What!?*" Kemia and Xathaniel exclaimed.

"I am not your father. I was your guardian, your protector, because of who your father is."

"*What!?*" three voices said in unison from the shadows. Kemia stood stock-still—in shock. Pyriel was very sure she did not hear all the angels talking at once, demanding answers from Pyriel.

Kemia looked deeply into Pyriel's eyes. He felt he was paralyzed. He sensed power surge through him. It felt like Asival's electric current going throughout his body. The hairs on his arms and legs were standing at attention.

"Answer me truthfully," Kemia said. "Who is my father?"

Before he could answer, in a sparkle of silver, Rafayal appeared.

"Am I late?" Rafayal said, gracing the group with a rare smile. Six sets of eyes faced the angel. "What? What did I do?" he asked.

Kemia folded her arms across her chest. "Rafe, I have a funny feeling you have a very interesting story to tell me." The power surge around the group began to lessen.

"Little sister, are you doing this?"

"Don't try to distract me."

"I am not." Rafayal looked from one angel to another. "Have you not felt the power that surrounded you? Kim, are you doing this?"

Xathaniel walked to Kemia's side and took her hand. "She is, sir. As her guardian, I take full responsibility. Kim is unaware of her blessings. We start training and practice tomorrow."

Rafayal dipped his head in acknowledgement. "Of course, you know what this means. Come. We must have a conference in private." The two angels walked across the roof, out of earshot. Pyriel watched as they walked away. He turned to find Kemia standing in front of him, six inches in front of him to be exact.

"You have a story to tell me, right?" she said.

"Do you not think we should chat at a later time? You have more pressing matters to attend to."

"Why would you say that?" Kemia asked, a little annoyed. Pyriel looked at her. Then it occurred to him why she was not in awe of Rafayal. She does not know Rafayal's position in heaven. Now he was left with more decisions on what to tell her.

"Excuse me, my Lady Kemia." Pyriel bowed formally to her and made his way over to Rafayal and Xathaniel.

Xathaniel nodded a greeting toward him but kept talking to Rafayal. "Sir, we are puzzled by the blood service placed on me."

"As am I. I will try to have more answers on the morrow. Is this the only reason for your call? Is Kim well?"

"She is now. I was concerned for a time. I mean no disrespect, but do you know who her parents are?" Xathaniel said.

Pyriel spoke up. "I came over to ask questions along the same lines. How much or little shall I tell her?"

Rafayal looked from one angel to the other. "I will speak to you both separately on the morrow. As for her parents, I never asked the whole story. I must seek the same answers you do."

Pyriel said in a quiet voice, "All these years I thought you were her father. Sir, what do I tell her?"

Three angels looked over to their subject. She was laughing and chatting with Peter. "Tell her the truth," Rafayal said. "You asked for answers and will seek them out."

"I will not mislead or tell untruth to my helpmate," Xathaniel said.

Rafayal graced them with another rare smile. "So you have decided."

"From first moment we talked." Xathaniel stood taller. "I am ready to fall once my service is complete."

Pyriel was stunned. "But you are an arc! Are you giving up service?"

Rafayal's hand came down on Pyriel's shoulder. "Be easy. We will meet on the morrow. Do not fret. I will take everything into my choosing." With those words, Rafayal disappeared as he had come.

"Do not tell Kemia of my decision to stay earthbound," Xathaniel said quietly. "She will think of nothing of sacrificing herself for a greater good. She still thinks her life force is ebbing and the power she is blessed with is temporary."

"You have my word."

"I am counting on it," Xathaniel said. He walked over and took Kemia's hand. They both waved at him and then disappeared in red sparks.

That is odd, Pyriel thought. *There is that red color again.*

"Are you well, Brother?" Asival's soft inquiry broke into his thoughts.

"I am well. However, I can feel that there is something on your mind."

"I had thought we had no secrets from one another."

"And we still do not."

"So what was all that with Kemia?" Pyriel could hear the anger in his twin's voice. "You are still holding back information, not only from her but from me as well."

Pyriel looked at his sister, willing her to understand. "I cannot share just yet. Know this: you will always be my confidant. That will never change. Understand that because of service, there are things I cannot share. Even from past service assignments."

Asival smiled. "I understand. Just so you understand that I would like answers at a later date."

"Understood. Peace be with you, Asival. I have much to contemplate."

"Peace be with you." She disappeared in a shower of silver sparks.

Pyriel closed his eyes. *What do I do now? I do not want to lose trust and friendships.*

Do not fret, Guardian. Just continue to trust those who are trustworthy.

Pyriel opened his eyes. Yes, he had much to think about.

CHAPTER 14

Nyssa Wallace was crying so hard, her vision blurred. It wasn't the slap across her face that had made her cry. It was the fact that she was at her mother and stepfather's mercy.

"I told you to do the laundry, and I wanted it done before I came home!" her stepfather yelled.

"Stanly, I had to go to work. If I don't work, I can't pay you and mom my room and board for the month." Before Nyssa could say another word, Stanly hit her a second time. This time his hand came across her face where her jaw and eye met. Her face felt like it was on fire at first, and then it became a throbbing ache.

"How many times have I told you to call me Daddy, girl? Still think I'm not good enough to be your daddy?" he yelled, even louder that before. His words were slurring together.

Oh, no! Nyssa thought with dismay. *Not again.* She wasn't sure if he was drunk, high, or both.

"Go upstairs, and wait in your room for your punishment," Stanly said with a sudden gleam in his eyes. She wasn't fooled. She knew what was coming. She knew it was useless to appeal to her mother, but she had to try.

"Mom, I cleaned the kitchen, dusted the living room, cleaned all the floors, and cleaned all the bedrooms. I was planning on doing the laundry tonight before bed."

Della McKinley watched her husband and daughter with bored fascination. "Don't involve me in any of this. You did something wrong, and you have to learn." Nyssa realized too late that Della was just as high as Stanly.

This is not good, Nyssa thought. Without another word, Nyssa tore up the stairs. She tried desperately to hold back the tears that threatened to come. Right now, she couldn't afford the luxury of crying. She had to hide the twins from her stepfather. She knew that just as God had created the heavens above, Stanly McKinley would head to the corner liquor store before he came up to "punish" her. Her punishment would consist of beatings, followed by rape. This had gone on long enough. For three years she had been subjected to him and his friends thinking they could take what they wanted. She had managed to fend off Stanly's friends, but she had no such fortune with Stanly. Sometimes she could keep away from him, but sometimes she had bad luck. At seventeen, she knew it was time to leave.

Of course, she couldn't leave the twins. Nyssa had recently found a secret hiding place in the basement. She was hiding from her stepfather in a small closet. It was a broom closet. Nyssa could barely fit. When Stanly gave up and left to get his drug fix, she exited the closet. What a loud clatter, a broom and a mop fell to the floor. When she bent down to pick them up, there was an envelope taped to the bottom corner of the door. Nyssa opened it. Inside she found a floor plan of the basement and a key. The twins could sleep there, safe and warm, until they all could escape.

As she reached the top of the landing, she knew they were hiding from their parents. She gave three quick raps on the wall. As if by magic, two six-year-old, identical twin boys appeared.

"Mathew, Sam, grab those things I packed yesterday." The boys scrambled to do their sister's bidding.

"Hurry boys. We don't have much time," she whispered urgently. "Be sure to take flashlights and some toys." The boys had everything in their backpacks. Nyssa took hold of their hands. Slowly, the children crept down the stairs. As they were taking their fourth step, Nyssa smelled something funny. It smelled like burning rocks. Then she heard voices. They froze in place on the stairs.

"Mr. McKinley, you promised to have the information we paid you handsomely for. Do you have it?" Nyssa motioned for the twins to stay quiet and still. They nodded that they understood. Nyssa slipped down two steps more. What greeted her was Stanly pinned to the floor by humanoid, shadow creatures. A beautiful woman was standing over him. Two more creatures had Della pinned to the sofa. The woman wasn't paying too much attention to Nyssa's mother. She was more interested in her stepfather and his answers.

"I'm very close. I was going to take my twins to the park and ask around."

The woman did not look pleased at Stanly's reply. She waved her left hand, and Stanly moaned in pain. For a brief moment, Nyssa was glad. For once, he would know what it was like for her and her brothers. It evaporated quickly when she saw what the woman did next. The woman was holding what looked like a snake, but it was long and pitch black.

"Please, Racheal," Stanly said. "I can do a better job."

"You've had three years, Mr. McKinley. It is too late to find another couple who is …" The woman, Racheal, smiled evilly and then continued. "Shall we say, truly diabolical. You rape and beat your daughter for pleasure." She turned to face Bella and another snakelike creature appeared in her other hand. "And you allow it. Here is something you may not know, *Mommy*. Do you know your husband has a bidding war going for your twins?"

"No! Not my babies!" Della cried. "You promised that if I let you have Nyssa you would leave my babies alone! You lied. *You lied! No!*" Della was screaming and crying. The two creatures had her pinned firmly to the sofa. Nyssa's parents were both struggling, but no matter how much they fought, they could not free themselves.

"Now." Racheal slowly approached Stanly. "You say the child in question is at the park every night with her mother?"

Stanly nodded.

"Are you sure she is the correct age?"

Again Stanly nodded.

"So is this the place where you give your boys to the highest bidder as well?"

This time Stanly didn't answer.

"No matter. I will get all my answers and control you at the same time."

Racheal stooped down and put one of the snake creatures on Stanly's chest. She walked over and placed one on Della's chest as well.

"All comfy and set?" Rachael said. "Let's begin again."

"Dells, keep your mouth closed."

"I don't want you to talk to me, you lying bas—" Nyssa saw the snake creature enter Della's mouth, cutting off her words. Della started hacking and coughing. After a few seconds, her eyes turned soot black and then went back to their natural color of topaz brown.

"Release her." The shadow creatures released Della, and she stood up. She remained standing without moving. "Now, Mr. McKinley, let us continue our playdate. You will get the child and deliver her to me in four days. Do I make myself clear, or do you need further explanation?"

Stanly glared at Racheal without saying a word.

Racheal just smiled. "Are we playing that game? Well, I was rather good at it." She studied her nails and said, "What if I take your plaything away? What would you do?" She was greeted by silence. "Oh, I would not stop there; I would take your wife away as well."

"You leave my Della alone, you bit—" The snake creature slid into Stanly's mouth. He gagged for a few seconds, and then his eyes turned black—but Stanly's eyes remained black; they did not return to his natural color of gray.

"Release him."

The humanoid creatures let Stanly up from the floor. He stood well over a foot taller than Racheal. Racheal frowned. "Four days. No more. If you fail me this time, I will not be so … nice. I will come back on the fourth day. Do not disappoint me. Good-bye, Mr. and Mrs. McKinley." Racheal dropped a sack of bills and a brown, wrapped package on the table and disappeared in a puff of black, rock-burning smoke.

Nyssa had had her fist shoved in her mouth, biting down to keep from crying out during the whole exchange. She felt something brush her side. She started to find both boys next to her. One look told her that they had seen it all. She placed her index finger against her lips to indicate that they should remain quiet. Three pairs of eyes turned toward their parents.

Della was the first one to move. She grabbed half of the stack of bills. "I'm going out. Be back tomorrow."

Stanly shook his head as if to clear it. His eyes were now gray with black rings. He reached for Della and latched onto her wrist. His six-foot-three body towered over her five-foot-five frame. "You can't go. You have to help me with the kid."

"*No!* You sold my babies after you promised!"

"I tell you what: help me with the kid, and I'll call off the sale."

Della frowned up at him. "How do I know you won't lie about that?"

Stanly pulled Della into his embrace. "Take the children to one of your friends' houses tomorrow, and don't tell me where they are for … say three weeks?"

Della thought for a moment and then answered. "Okay. Deal. What do you want me to do tonight?"

"I'll show you the park and the kid we need to get. Pretend you lost your dog."

"We don't have a dog."

"I'll take care of that. C'mon."

Stanly dragged Della out the back door. When the children heard the back door slam shut, they quickly made their way to the basement. Nyssa shut the basement door firmly behind her and her brothers. She flipped on one of the flashlights.

"Hang on to my shirt, boys."

She descended the stairs, making her way to the far right corner of the basement. In front of her was a door leading up and out to the backyard. She turned and faced the wall to her immediate right. She took out a tiny key. In passing, one might mistake it for a diary key. Nyssa pushed at a small section of the wall. The false piece of the wall lifted to reveal a lock. Nyssa inserted her key and turned it clockwise until she heard it click. Then she turned it counterclockwise. The wall opened with a soft snick to share its secret—a twelve-by-twelve room with a queen-sized bed in the corner.

Inside the room was a bookshelf crammed with supplies, bottled water, canned goods, and preboxed, ready-to-eat snacks. In the center of the room was a coffee table with a lantern, puzzles, and board games. Nyssa gently pushed the twins forward. She closed and locked the door behind her. On this side of the door, she only had to flip the mechanism. She replaced the key around her neck. Next, she walked over to the wall that housed the window and stood on a plastic milk crate to reach the latch of the window to let in some fresh air. She climbed down, walked over to the bedside table, and clicked on the table lamp. She took a sheer, colored scarf and covered the lampshade. From the outside, the window would look like the wall to the house as long as strong light did not shine through. Nyssa had planted flowers and a couple of bushes outside to ensure extra privacy.

If things worked out, she and the boys would be able to leave in one week. One more week and she would be able to put the boys in a private school for one year. She would serve a year in the military and get a household set up. The plan wasn't perfect, but it would do. She turned to find the twins right where she left them. Samuel was humming a tuneless tune, and Mathew was standing next to his brother, rocking both of them. Nyssa looked at her brothers and recognized the signs of distress. She went over to them, wrapped her arms around them both, and lifted them up. She danced them round the room as she hummed along with Sam. Matthew was the first to giggle; Samuel followed. Nyssa crashed onto the bed, taking the twins with her. The children's laughter was free and light.

"So, do you guys like our clubhouse?" she said breathlessly. "I've been working on it all week."

Samuel was the first to speak. "Nyssa, is this the place you promised to take us?"

"No, sweetie. I'm still working on that. This is so you two don't have to hide under your beds or lock yourselves in your closet. You'll be safe. They don't know about this place. So it has to be our secret—promise?"

"We promise," they said in unison.

"Issa?"

"Yes, peaches."

"What were those things that Mommy and Daddy swallowed?" Nyssa looked down into the serious eyes of Samuel.

Samuel was different from most children. When she took the boys to the park, Sam would play alone. Matthew would play with the other children for a little while, and then he would spend time with his brother.

Matthew was the creative one of the two. Samuel was the practical one. On more than one occasion she had found Samuel taking apart electronic devices. Just the previous week, Samuel had taken apart the coffee maker and vacuum. When Nyssa questioned Sam on what he was doing, he simply responded that he needed the parts. She had looked questioningly at Matthew. Matthew had said that they were building a time machine.

Nyssa knew she needed to replace the appliances before her parents discovered they were missing. She had worked a double shift, doing her homework during her breaks at work. She hoped to be able to replace them in a few days. But it was little too late.

Stanly had wanted to make coffee a few days earlier, and when he questioned the boys about the missing appliance, Matthew informed him that they had taken it to build something. That night, when Nyssa had come home from work, she found Matt in bed, barely moving, and Sam by his side, humming and rocking in his distress. Nyssa could hear Della and Stanly arguing and fighting in their bedroom.

Nyssa had instantly put three rubber bands around Sam's wrist. He began to snap and play with the bands. "Come, Sam." She had lifted Matt gently and headed to her room. Once there, she laid Matt on her bed and shut and locked her door. As an extra precaution, Nyssa moved her bed in front of the door and pushed her dresser behind the headboard. Sam was still playing with the rubber bands, but he was no longer rocking. He was still humming. He was looking at his brother.

Nyssa immediately examined Matt. What she found were bruises on his stomach, legs, and back. No broken bones. Nyssa sighed in relief. Matthew had shut his mind down and crawled into himself. She didn't know how or when he learned to do that, but she knew how to bring him back. She ran to her bathroom and wet a washcloth with cold water, and then she proceeded to wipe Matt's face. She spoke to him, willing him to come back, telling him he was safe. After ten minutes, Matt slowly sat up.

Right then and there, she had vowed to have a safe place for them when she was not home.

Presently, she did not think anywhere in the house would be safe. After seeing her parents and the shadow creatures, no matter how painful, she knew she had to leave this week instead of in two months as she had planned.

Sam was waiting patiently for Nyssa to answer about the shadow creatures. "I don't know," she told him.

"Listen." Above their heads, they heard Stanly return. The children huddled together on the bed. Nyssa rocked them to and fro and whispered, "You're safe." She said it over and over again. "I'm not going to let them hurt you."

Stanly walked into the house chuckling. Della was really stupid if she thought he was going to give up all that money for her. She spent four hundred dollars a day just shopping, and another five hundred dollars on drugs. She refused to work. And the twenty grand that Racheal had brought them was chump change. So far, he had been offered fifty grand for one of those brats, and as of thirty minutes ago, the bid was at ninety-five thousand for the pair.

No, he was definitely not calling off the sale. The buyer wanted updated footage of the twins and proof that the boys were indeed six years old, not sixteen, before he deposited half the funds in Stanly's account. The other half would be given to him in cash at the time of the exchange. So far, his plan of selling the twin boys was right on schedule. He knew his wife would protest, but he had her busy getting chummy with the little girl's mother so that they could take her tomorrow night.

Meanwhile, he needed to take footage of the boys holding today's newspaper. He placed the paper and a bottle of whiskey on the table. He knew the little boys were terrified of him. That's what he liked, the fear. He craved it. Since Racheal had put that shadow bug in him, he craved it even more. He made sure everyone he encountered feared him one way or another, including his wife—although, Della would never admit it.

Stanly frowned. There was one person who did not fear him. That was his stepdaughter. The first time he raped her, she had been a virgin. He did it to get her fear; after that, it became a challenge to get as much fear from her. Then he discovered a different fear. It was more powerful than anything he had ever felt. It was fear for someone you loved more than yourself.

Remembering it brought a deep craving. It was more addicting than the meth he smoked or the brown liquor he consumed.

You know what we want, Mr. McKinley. We want the dark, black feeling. We want the fear; we want the darkness. We are hungry. The shadow bug was speaking to him. He had no resistance against it. It knew his thoughts before Stanly could fully formulate them.

Stanly sat on the sofa, opened the bottle of whiskey, and took a long pull. "Patience," he told it. "You do want it to be good, right?"

We do. We want much. We want all.

Stanly listened to sounds of the house. It wasn't unusual to find the house so silent. He took a deep breath. Nyssa. He could smell her. She insisted on using jasmine soap and perfume. She refused to use any other scent.

Ah, it was time.

Finally. We are hungry. Feed us. Feed us! the shadow bug screamed.

Stanly held his head in his hand for a few minutes before he got up and slammed the empty bottle onto the spotless table. Time to stir up fear. He staggered up the stairs, making as much noise as possible.

"Time to be punished, girl!" he shouted up the stairs. Stanly chuckled as he made his way to Nyssa's bedroom. He stood in front of her door and then suddenly kicked it open. "Where are you, girl? I know you and those brats are hiding." He yanked open trunks, upturned beds, and ripped through closets with all the anger that was bottled up. Stanly tore through her room, and once he did that, he made his way into her bathroom and yanked back the shower curtain. Empty.

"Come on, little girl; there are only so many places you can hide," he called. He tore through the boys' room with the same purpose.

No! They are gone! Stanly thought with despair. His money would be gone then too.

No, said the shadow bug. *They are not gone. Feel her? Feel her fear for her brothers? Feel the fear of the children? So pure, so intoxicating. Follow it. Trace it. Go.*

Stanly stood in the middle of the upstairs landing.

Concentrate. Let us lead you. We are hungry.

He was surprised by what felt like an electrical shock that traveled throughout his whole body. Then, he smelled them. Not just Nyssa's soap but their fear. All of sudden, he was hungry. The air attacked him with smells of steak with fried onions, fries, and apple pie. That was his favorite meal!

Yes, Mr. McKinley, follow the smells. Stanly tore down the stairs.

He paused in the living room. "Are you here? You are going to pay for messing with my money!" he shouted to the air.

Oh yeah, she will pay. After tonight, Nyssa would have outlived her usefulness. She had kept those brats quiet and fed. Stanly had to admit, she did know how to cook, and she had kept the four-bedroom, three-bath home spotless. For the past eight years, he delighted in having a live-in slave. He refused to see her as anything else. But tonight was the night. Unfortunately, he would have to get rid of Della as well.

Yesssssssss. You must. We will bring you a new wife, one with other children to sell. Take care of this first. We are hungry.

Nyssa, Matthew, and Samuel listened to Stanly bang and thump upstairs. At one point they heard glass breaking. Nyssa flinched. Her crystal glass collection. He finally destroyed it. Her father had bought them for her before he died. Each one was given to her with meaning and love, from the winged warrior angels to the horses. Whenever Nyssa thought about her father, she felt a comforting warmth in her heart. But this time, it was different. The warmth was there as usual, but this time it was stronger.

Young guardian, you must take your charges and run. Now! I will protect you as much as possible. Run! Now!

Nyssa whispered to the boys, "We must go. Right now, boys. He's coming for us. Matt, stack those crates over by the window. Sam, please grab those bags in the corner. Hurry, boys. Hurry." She ran over to the bookshelf and reached toward the back on the middle shelf. She pulled out a can of shaving cream. Nyssa turned the top and then the bottom of the can. The can gave way to her money stash. She knew $973 was not going to last long. But it was a start. She turned to find the boys waiting for her next set of instructions.

"Listen very carefully. I'm going to lift you up through the window; if I am not out in five minutes, take the bags I packed and yourselves to Justus Hunter's house. Do you remember where he lives?" Both boys nodded silently. Nyssa heard Stanly coming down the basement stairs.

Hurry, Guardian, they are almost upon you. Nyssa grabbed Sam first and lifted him through the window. She then did the same with Matt. She zipped the money into one of the bags along with a note. She then handed the three overnight bags up to the twins. At first she was concerned that the bags were too heavy for them. But they took them up with no problem. Nyssa climbed down from the crates and proceeded to set traps in the room. She wound a rope on hooks on the back of the bookshelves and through others attached underneath the tables. She tied the rope to the top crate stacked at the window. She gave one last look around. "Good-bye, Daddy. I love you." It felt right to say that. It felt comforting to say good-bye to her father's house that way.

Guardian, you are out of time. They have found you. They plan to end your life force.

Nyssa climbed up the crates and squeezed out the window. She did not know how she knew, but she understood what the voice was talking about.

Young guardian, do not activate your plan. There are spies. Go to the hotel with the flashing stars. She didn't fully trust the voice. She would trust her instinct. It was what had kept her and the twins one step ahead of Stanly for years. Her instinct told her to follow the voice's advice.

She put all of the bags on herself and took the hands of her brothers. Nyssa walked as quickly as she could. She flagged down a taxi, after all, they were all over New York, and she gave the man the name of a hotel one block away from her destination.

She hoped and prayed this would work.

CHAPTER 15

Xathaniel and Kemia had been practicing her blessings for two hours. They had distracted the other angels with food. Kemia had introduced them to a buffet and a video arcade. Then she and Xathaniel went to a nearby field on the outskirts of the city. So far, Kemia had managed to control her emotions that projected her power source. Xathaniel sighed. He needed to make sure she had mastered that. He still did not know what news Pyriel and Rafayal had to give. He had had to draw her back four times the night before. *She might do harm to others, if not herself,* he thought.

Kemia's voice broke into his thoughts. "Nate, we have been at this for hours." Kemia frowned and then brightened with an idea. "When are we going to test the kissing stuff?"

Xathaniel laughed. "That, my dear Fire, will be the last item on our practice list."

Xathaniel felt warmth and power move through him. *Warrior guardian, help them. The children need your help.*

"Kemia, we have to go this instant!"

"What's wrong?"

"We have been summoned."

"*Wow!* My very first assignment. How exciting! Let's go," she said. She ran into his arms, and in a flash of silver, they appeared at their hotel. When they arrived, they saw two police cars; the officers and the hotel manager were arguing.

"When I checked them in, they had adults with them. I made sure. You can't fine me if their parents deserted them!" The manager waved his arms angrily. Three children were sitting on the curb—a girl of sixteen or seventeen and twin boys who looked to be four or five. The girl had her arms protectively around the smaller children. They were being questioned by a couple of detectives. There was a fire of defiance in the girl's eyes.

Xathaniel tipped his head to the side. *She looks like Kim,* he thought.

Power and warmth came over him again. *She is called Nyssa, and she is a guardian that must be trained. Go to them.*

"I'll be right back," Xathaniel said, but he felt a tug on the back of his shirt. He turned to find the other angels.

"So, we have to train her?" Peter asked. "I have never trained before. Has anyone noticed how much she looks like Lady Kemia?"

Avial hit Peter on the back of the head. "Thanks, Captain Obvious."

"Ow! I was just saying—"

"All right—enough, you guys." Kemia laughed. "Let's go get our charge." The group made their way over to the children and the detectives.

"Young lady, I am *not* going to ask you again," the detective was saying. "Where do you live? Where are the adults you checked in with?" The girl remained stubbornly silent. Kemia cleared her throat to get the detective's attention.

"Perhaps we could help." The startled detective was stricken speechless for a moment. After his partner nudged him for a second time, he spoke.

"Who might you be?"

Kemia smiled. "I might be her sister, and these are my stepbrothers."

The other detective spoke up. "We have been trying to get their names and address from them for fifteen minutes now. We got a call this morning that they were runaways. Their father is on his way to identify his children."

"That's impossible, sir. We have no parents. I went to find work and left them with a babysitter," Kemia explained. She continued in a stage whisper. "I went off on one of my jobs. I'm a photographer, you see, and I left them with a couple who I thought would care for them. They were abusive, so I came to take them back to my new home. We stopped here for the night. I left this morning to find work."

"Well, you do look alike, and the man at the station looks nothing like the children. If we could get the children to …" The detective trailed off. He noted that the twin boys no longer looked frightened.

One boy was chasing and playing tag with a blond-haired man. The other was writing and talking to another man who looked like he'd just left the military. The young girl stood silently next to the woman who was talking to him. The detective looked over at his partner. His partner shrugged. "Well, they do look like they are familiar with you. Ma'am, may I see some ID, please?"

"Sure." Kemia reached in her handbag and pulled out her wallet.

"Please pull it out of the billfold."

"No problem. Here you go." Kemia handed him the proper documents. "Will there be anything else?"

After both detectives looked over her ID and handed it back to her, the one who'd asked for her ID responded. "No. We'll take care of the man claiming to be the father. Is this your proper address?"

"It is, Officer. May we leave?"

"Sure." Both detectives watched the woman round up her companions. "What a nice family. Let's go meet this McKinley guy and get the real story on him."

As soon as they were out of earshot of the detectives and police officers, Kemia said quietly, "We need to meet in my room." She turned to the girl. "Is that okay, Guardian Nyssa?"

"How do you know my name?"

Kemia looked around to assure they were alone. *Flash us all to the roof, Nate.* She spoke to him in his mind.

Xathaniel was only slightly surprised. "As you wish, Kim," he said out loud. In a flash, the whole party was on the roof in the same spot as the night before. Peter had one boy on each hip. They didn't look like they had any intentions of climbing down. Pyriel and Asival stood to his left, and Avial stood on the right. Nyssa was standing in front of Kemia and Xathaniel.

"Now, I think introduction are in order," Kemia began.

"Why did you call me guardian? The voice in my head called me the same thing. Who are you?"

Avial bowed at Nyssa. "Young guardian, we were sent to train you to continue to protect your charges. Avial at your service."

In a flash of silver light, Rafayal appeared. He did not speak to the angels but went directly to Nyssa. "You made it."

"You're the voice that told me to run yesterday."

"I am. Your father and mother were my guardians. They would have been so proud to know you are a guardian as well." Rafayal, to the surprise of all who were present, embraced Nyssa. Power could be seen around both of them. "I am glad to have found you at last, Goddaughter."

The angels exchanged puzzled looks.

"Rafe, I hate to interrupt, but you have a lot of explaining to do." Kemia sounded more than a little annoyed.

Rafayal pulled back from hugging Nyssa. "Yes. There is much to discuss. You must take Nyssa and her two charges, Matthew and Samuel, with you to the first garden. Nyssa must be trained on the way. I call to service Pyriel and Asival."

Asival did not like being pushed around. She felt like she was on a chessboard being maneuvered to suit. "And why should we? You have secrets, and you are keeping them from us. We deserve to know what is going on!"

"Quiet, Sister."

Rafayal faced Pyriel. "You know—do you not?"

"Yes. I was there during the council's decree."

"She is one of them. She has been moved and erased 243 times."

"Wait. I don't understand." Nyssa's eyes widened.

"Give it a few minutes for the healing to take effect. Nyssa, you are over 150 years old. You guard the child that will possibly end this war," Rafayal said softly.

Power sparked from Kemia. "Dark ones are here for us. We must go."

"Yes. We will meet you in three days. Look for a town named for an earthly saint." With those words, Rafayal disappeared in a shower of power.

Xathaniel look down the side of the roof to find a man covered in a very dark aura hanging around the front of the hotel. He could feel the shadows around him. "Rafe is correct. We must go now."

Rafayal hurried to Mycheal's office. Without pausing at Zophael's desk, he continued on and entered Mycheal's inner office. Without preamble, he said, "It has begun."

Mycheal looked up from his work. "Are you sure?"

"I found Katlyn and Adam's child."

Mycheal jumped up. "*No!* That is wonderful news, my friend!"

"There is more. She has been guardian to the child."

Mycheal look stunned. "We must make preparations. It will not be long before it is known."

"One more thing. I researched Lady Kemia."

"Okay. And?"

Rafayal took a deep breath and sighed. "She wants to know who her parents are."

"So tell her. Finding her human parents should not be hard."

"She is only half human."

"She is of unpure blood, wielding that kind of power?"

"Yes, but she is pure blood. I have healed her. I saw."

"Things are changing."

"They are. Let us get the other two. We must prepare for battle."

Rafayal felt the power in his blood surge.

GLOSSARY

Names

Xathaniel – \Nathaniel/
Kemia – \Ke ma/
Rafayal – \Raf fae al/
Mycheal – \Mik cal/
Danjal – \Dan yal/
Gabriel – \Ga bri el/
Pyriel – \Py ral/
Avial – \A vile/
Asival – \As e vil/
Calinda – \Cal lenda/
Zophael – \Zo fe al/
Azazel – \Az a zel/
Kadosh – \Kay dosh/
Arvial – \Are ve al/

Terms

blessing – Gifts given to do service
service/to service – Duty or assignment
blood service – An assignment that if not done properly, or at all, a life force will be taken
life force – The life and spirit of a being

service gauntlets – Wristbands worn by angels in service
power source – Universal power
summon/to summon – A call to an assignment
missive/missives – Written messages
first garden – Garden of Eden